[COLOR PLATES]

"*Color Plates* is a breakthrough collection. I could not put this book down. Like all lovers of contemporary fiction, I hunt for that rare and intelligent voice that both inspires and delights—Golaski is that voice. A trickster more deft than Steven Millhauser, Golaski is a visionary wordsmith and *Color Plates* is a wonder box of stories. Not only will I buy this book for my friends and relatives, I will carry *Color Plates* around with me to spark my own imagination and writing—a one-of-a-kind book find, a mind-blowing reading experience. I love this book."

—Debra Magpie Earling, author of *Perma Red*

"The haunted, haunting tales in Adam Golaski's *Color Plates* share a painterly attention to 'quick application, short strokes' and the same idiosyncratic, off-kilter take on narrative as the canvases by Manet, Degas, Cassatt, and Toulouse-Lautrec this book invokes. These brief stories invent and re-invent worlds: as the book itself has it, 'they start one way and go another.'"

—Joshua Harmon, author of *Quinnehtukqut* and *Scape*

"In this doubly ekphrastic collection, busy, vertiginous worlds open up from the two dimensions of a painted canvas, or the still more meager resources of the printed page: family upon family, girlfriend after girlfriend, inverting hills, a collapsing balcony, a retreating shoreline, a sleeping projectionist and a slipping picture, shadow boxes and cast parties, carousel horses and paper jockeys, baths and mirrors, doubles and trains, grass green, lamp green, jade green, & dress green. Each painting opens up onto prose, each prose opens up into a kind of chambered flux, and, on such ingenious axes, human figures flex, dip, and leap like tiny tumblers."

—Joyelle McSweeney, author of *Flet* and *Nylund, the Sarcographer*

[COLOR PLATES]

Adam Golaski

Rose Metal Press

2010

Rose Metal Press, Inc.
P.O. Box 1956
Brookline, MA 02446
rosemetalpress@gmail.com
www.rosemetalpress.com

Library of Congress Control Number: 2010932007

ISBN: 978-0-9846166-0-2

Cover and interior design by Melissa Gruntkosky
Interior typeface: ITC Slimbach

Cover art: *outside my window, in the dark* by Dan McCarthy
More info and images can be viewed at his website: www.danmccarthy.org.

This book is manufactured in the United States of America and printed on acid-free paper.

  This book was sponsored in part by grants from the National Endowment for the Arts and the Massachusetts Cultural Council.

[CONTENTS]

book two:
EDGAR DEGAS
PLATES 20–33

book three:
HENRI DE TOULOUSE-LAUTREC
PLATES 34–50

book four:
MARY CASSATT
PLATES 51–66

acknowledgments

I am grateful to the editors who published individual *Color Plates* in their journals; their support was crucial to the completion of this project. Different (sometimes radically so) versions of the following plates appeared as recorded here: "Cirque Fernando" in *Triggering*; "The Grand Loge" and "A Corner in the Moulin de la Galette" in *Hanging Loose*; "La Goulue Entering the Moulin Rouge," "At the Moulin Rouge," and "The Toilette" in *Supernatural Tales*; "Head of a Young Woman," "Spartan Boys and Girls Exercising," "The Dancing Class" (1876 & 1880), "The Mante Family," "Woman Fixing Her Stocking," "The Modiste," and "The Cup of Tea" in *Lit*; "Head of a Young Girl," "Reading *Le Figaro*," "Little Girl in a Blue Armchair," and "Study for At the Opera" in *Web Conjunctions*; "Boating at Argenteuil" in *Sleepingfish*; "Prologue: Portrait of the Artist" in *Absent*; and "The Cotton Market, New Orleans," "The Bellelli Family," and "The Café Singer" in *McSweeney's;* "Boy with Cherries" in *Smokelong Quarterly.*

The writings of art historians Sam Hunter, S. Lane Faison, Jr., Daniel Catton Rich, and Nancy Mowll Mathews were of great use to me during the writing of this book.

My love to those who were with me in and out of the book, without whom there would be no *Color Plates.* Thank you Sharma Shields, Sam Mills, and Kaethe Schwehn. Thanks to Danielle Marie Winterton for her especial editorial enthusiasm. The Blue Poets—John, Matthew, Jeff, and Jaime. Winter ("Baby Reaching for an Apple") & Nico. Conrad & Louise—for the childhood they made for me and my sister. Elizabeth asks, "We are family?"—yes we are. And Zetta & Elizabeth, I'm so glad.

for Marie

"Portrait of the Artist"

1878, 24 x 18

My name is Mary and Mary is my museum. Paintings are brushstroke upon brush-stroke. With a pencil I lift each brushstroke and make lines. Finally. What I leave behind is my body—a portrait.

Old and small: that is how my body left me. I spent such a long time dreaming. Visits from people I knew well and loved and from people I didn't know I loved. Simone, in a wizard's hat. Brown cloak with yellow felt stars glued along the hem. Though I spoke with you only once, twice, Simone—I love you. The incredible eyes of Joseph, one yellow, one red—the colors shifting from one eye to the other. Joseph, your eyes. My portrait: a white dress, a hat piled with flowers, my body posed to look out-of-pose. I was humble enough not to look up, out, beyond the scrim of brushstrokes. The artist could only have been Mary, myself; those aren't my brushstrokes anymore. An apart-ment much larger than the apartment I lived in for all those years, ten, twenty. My grandfather dying. I stood by his bed and I thought then, I'll soon be old and dying too. To be young as I still was when I stood by my grandfather, when I posed for my portrait. I cannot be young anymore. My sister, Lydia, seven months pregnant with her first child, a window behind her, wind lifting tree branches up — rain danced against the side of the house for just under a half hour.

I drift beyond my heart, on out of dream into space. I see what I think must be other galaxies but is our galaxy, this galaxy. At the ends of space are mirrors. What once we thought were other galaxies is only this galaxy, circling at the head of a staircase, looking down to a door kept locked. Simone, you step through that door without opening it — magic — and you climb the stairs. You don't look up, the peak of your wizard's hat a point, a moon, a star. Where I've kept Simone's face is a mystery; she'd been forgotten from my life. I am with you, Joseph, days *before* I met you. He acts as he did before he knew me (but he believed I existed, without evidence; his joy when his belief was confirmed upon our meeting transformed into love). I see Joseph, my husband, before he was my husband, when he was a high school student. He sat behind Anna, on whom he had a terrible crush during his senior year. I feel his crush — Anna, you were so lovely. Joseph, a little boy, sitting on the ground, dust in his hair. A gift, a Heaven, to see things from my life that I never saw. In space, the other galaxies are glass and light. From darkness: like the glint of a deer's eye on a dark road I see God in the distance.

book one
ÉDOUARD MANET

[PLATE 1]

"Boy with Cherries"

1858, 25 ¾ x 21 ½

Red: hat, fruit, face and hands. Reds in the brown background and coat. Reds in the green; the wall that is green and the lettuce leaves. Manet's studio was dark. He was well liked by men and women, for different reasons, though he was taciturn and apt to take a razor to any canvas that bore a likeness he did not admire. Here is a boy with cherries and yet only the smallest areas of canvas are illuminated.

Brother and Sister drive out of a small northern California town. Yellow dust rises around their rental car. The sky is pale blue. The median strip of brown grass is on fire; a controlled burn. The road is surrounded by fields of cherry trees.

"They're selling cherries on the side of the road," Brother says.

"They do that this time of year."

"We have to buy some."

Sister slows the car and pulls over. Brother gets out. The heat from the brush fire is intense. The smoke smells good though, clean like dirt.

Behind a low stone wall that's crumbled at either end is a chubby, pale boy. He wears what looks like a bellhop's hat. In front of him, on the stone wall the boy uses as a vendor's booth, are cherries, deep red and golden yellow cherries, displayed on broad and wilted lettuce leaves.

Brother asks, "How much for a bag of cherries?"

The boy speaks, mouths the price, and Brother can't tell for a moment if the boy is a boy or a midget; then he's sure he's a boy. Brother buys the cherries and gets back in the car with Sister.

With the bag of cherries between Brother's feet, Brother says, "Do you remember when Mom took us to meet up with Dad in the hotel in New York?"

"Um—"

"The one near the Chrysler Building?"

"I remember the Chrysler Building." She smiles. "I remember the new dress I wore."

"Do you remember the room we were in?"

"Not really." Sister sneaks a cherry from the bag and pops it into her mouth. The cherry is hot from the sun.

"It was adjacent to Mom and Dad's room. Remember? They used to do that. We would share a room and they would share a room, with a door that connected the two rooms."

"They did that all the time."

"They kept it unlocked in case we got scared. As always, you fell asleep right away. The room was dark and quiet—the ceiling was really low. I did fall asleep, eventually. But I had a bad dream and woke up. Really confused, like you are when you wake up in a strange place.

"I got out of bed and went straight to the door separating our rooms. I opened it and on the bed in the other room were a man and a woman who looked like our parents in all respects except that they were small.

"They got off the bed—they kind of bounced off, you know, like when you're a kid and the bed's just enormous."

"Sure."

"They asked if I was okay but I was dumbstruck, I couldn't remember why I was there and all I wanted to know was what had happened to Mom and Dad.

"The small man who looked like Dad pointed down to a spot on the bed, where I could see he had a collection of marbles. He picked up one marble — it was red — and another that was also red. His face was small, his body was small, his fingers were small. He knocked the marbles together — click, click — and the small woman who looked like our mother said, 'You see? There's no reason to be upset.' They smiled and smiled and finally I backed out of the room, back into our room. I got deep under the covers and I was glad you were there. Eventually I fell asleep."

"It was a dream?"

"Nope."

"Did you go into the wrong room?"

"I guess, something like that."

Sister gives Brother a sideways glance. "Did that really happen, Brother?"

"Sure it did."

Brother points to the side of the road. "Is that another cherry seller?"

Sister doesn't bother to look. "Out here, Brother, they're nothing special."

[PLATE 2]

"Luncheon on the Grass"

1863, 84 ½ x 106 ¼

A scandal of brushwork flusters the foliage, green and golden. The nude Victorine illuminates the canvas with her pale face and bones. A basket of fruit, scattered: cherries march toward a baguette like ants. No one can translate the French title "Le Déjeuner sur l'herbe." *There is no translation. Manet called the painting* "Le Bain" *because even in French,* "Le Déjeuner sur l'herbe" *cannot be translated.*

For a while, I thought about the first pearl ever discovered. Discovered inside an oyster shell brought up from clear water. The oily stone, found after the rough shell was split for shucking. The boy who brought up that first pearl surely knew it was valuable, but not like a coin, like a sea-smoothed piece of wood or the abandoned husk of a beetle. That boy put the pearl in a tree hollow, his alien jewel, only to be gazed at in secret.

I held one of the two women's pearls between my thumb and index finger — a pearl fitted with a gold spike for a pierced ear. I was a little late.

One of the women was standing in the pond. She wore only her slip. She was bent at the waist. Ringlets of water radiated from around her wrist as she reached for something she saw in the water.

The other woman lay on the grass naked, still damp from her skinny dip. Her confidence in her looks was notorious. Her clothes and the dress and shoes of the woman who stood in the pond lay rumpled behind her. She looked at me and smiled, because I was her target this afternoon. Soon, she planned, she would put on her clothes, a show that would make her irresistible.

Two men, my co-workers, who'd surely taken a car together, were seated on a blanket, still dressed in their suits. One of the men, who I often saw at the office, held the cane that he carried around but didn't use. He made a point to the other man, a friend of mine — an office friend — who wore his beard like an Amish farmer. My friend with the Amish beard looked at me and smiled a small smile that said, "I haven't been listening all afternoon" and "Look at our good fortune."

Trees grew on the shore and in the pond. Water lapped against an empty rowboat drawn up on a grassy knot. Shade fell around us but light illuminated our skin. Here and there, petals of pink hyacinth, on the bushes, in the water.

I upstaged the nude woman, and silenced the man with the cane, and caught my office friend by surprise: I stripped off my suit. Naked, I said, "I'm sorry I'm late" and "Is this anyone's pearl?" A pearl earring. I held it by its gold spike.

At that very moment, the woman in the slip also held up an object to the party. "Look at this stone," she said. "Isn't it the most marvelous stone anyone has ever seen?"

My co-workers, the nude woman and the woman with the stone — along with the picnic, the grove, the pond — were reflected on the surface of the pearl. The earring belonged to the woman who stood in the pond. She'd lost it in my car one evening, after a show.

"Olympia"

1863, 51½ x 73¾

Even if the model here is not Victorine, but a prostitute posing to arouse her client, she is Victorine. Her heeled slippers, her bow, pink as nothing, her brass bracelet and her black-ribbon-with-bell—the flowers delivered by Olympia's maid are for whomever Manet loved at that moment and that is why some are black and some so pale.

Of course you know the story of the woman who always wore a black ribbon around her neck. You know the story as it goes, as one version goes, that version which has her fall in love with a decent man, who puts up with the mystery of the black ribbon. ("Why do you wear that black ribbon?" he asks, over and over—on the day they met, on the day he proposed and she accepted, on their wedding day. And every time he asks she says, "I cannot tell you, my love.") The man who put up with the mystery of the black ribbon for so long one day can bear the mystery no longer and, depending on the effect the storyteller wishes for, he either releases the ribbon while she sleeps and her head tumbles from her neck, or, he and she are in the midst of a disagreement, and the ribbon becomes for him the cause of all their arguments, so he yanks the ribbon free, and her head drops to the floor, where he watches, in horror, as her head silently mouths a final reproach.

You have heard that story of the woman who wore the black ribbon around her neck. At the core of that version is the truth: there was a young woman who wore a black ribbon around her neck and when that ribbon was untied her head did fall off, bloodless, clean, as if it were the head of a porcelain doll.

Understand this: a woman with only a black ribbon standing between her and decapitation is cursed.

The question a reader ought to ask once the fact of her curse occurs to them is: *why is she cursed,* or, at the very least, *how did she come to be cursed?*

Let me describe for you a scene.

There is a heavy woman with a bouquet of flowers in her arms. She's wearing a dowdy pink dress, huge to cover her enormous breasts, her broad stomach, her great rear end. Her skin is very dark, black, so black that her head is almost invisible against the black curtain behind her. She is nearly as black as the ribbon. Her eyes, their dim yellows, their black pupils, are fixed on a woman who sits undressed, sits up in bed and gazes at nothing. She is the woman who wears a black ribbon around her neck, the cursed woman. Her skin is so pale it's as if she's dead.

The woman with the bouquet is not only gazing at the woman with the black ribbon around her neck. She is also transforming into a black cat, tail raised high, eyes human. The woman with the bouquet is transforming into a black cat and back into a woman so quickly it appears as if there is a black cat standing, hackles raised, at the foot of the bed and a woman with a bouquet gazing at the woman with the black ribbon around her neck. The black curtain that surrounds the bed ripples, disturbed by the wind that the woman with the bouquet generates as she transforms: faster and faster.

During, or through, that rapid transformation, a fine sheet of glass, thin like a candy ribbon, severs the neck of the woman on the bed. All that holds the woman's head to her body is the black ribbon she wore that day, tied around her neck that morning in a moment of fancy.

She tied that black ribbon around her neck while seated at her vanity. The ribbon originally was tied around a box of candy a suitor had given her, a box of candy she had opened at her vanity the night before. From the ribbon dangled a little brass bell. Now the bell dangles just over the soft spot where her neck meets her torso. The bell jingles wherever the woman walks, like a bell on a cat's collar.

The box of candy was a gift from the suitor who wed the woman with the black ribbon around her neck, and though he asked her many times throughout the course of their courtship, and after, during their marriage, "Why do you wear that black ribbon?" he asked only out of perversity. He knew. He had paid the woman with the bouquet of flowers, the woman who could transform into a cat, to put the curse on the woman with the ribbon around her neck.

You might wonder why he wanted her cursed, and why he would marry her then, and why he would untie the ribbon himself, but that I'll let you work out for yourselves: *what are the reasons*; ask.

You might have guessed that when people asked how his wife had wound up beheaded, he blamed the woman who could transform herself into a cat, "that black woman," he said, "that witch." And as you likely guessed, that poor explanation was enough to satisfy most people.

Then you will need to be reminded of an old wives' tale (as they call them): how cats can steal the breath from a man while he sleeps.

[PLATE 5]

"Portrait of Emile Zola"

1868, 57¼ x 43¼

*Objects in this picture refer to interests which Manet and Zola shared. Goya lurks
behind these Spanish pictures that Manet painted before he went to Spain. Further
blurring the intersection of these artists, the face of this portrait less resembles Zola,
than Manet.*

Emile read with a concentration most soothing. His office, quiet. Above his desk,
pinned to a corkboard, were little art prints and photos cut from the journal to which
he subscribed. These pictures overlapped one another. His desktop was a clutter of
books, papers, and pens. Against the wall, a row of handy volumes: reference books
and books he hoped to one day read.

He was seated at his desk to write, but instead took up an attractive and thick history he'd many times poked at and now procrastinated with—anything was more
interesting than the writing task at hand.

Emile's concentration balanced percolating ideas for what needed to be written
with the book's absorbing historical anecdotes he perused—the dual biographies, the
military strategies; but that balance was lost when a phrase he read catalyzed a new

and most singular line of thought. With a glaze upon his face, Emile looked up—his concentration now changed, not soothing but active and thoroughly engrossing. He was gone, gone into it—

How could a bullet kill?

What harm, a bullet?

A bullet would travel through him, a tiny package of molecules to slip between the field of his own molecules. Would, for a time, join with his molecules—his molecules would part . . .

No. He knew what damage a bullet would cause. Loss of blood, the shattering of bone, the destruction of organs, the likely, subsequent infection that would blaze outward from the locus of the bullet to ends of his extremities. Yet . . . , "Why," he thought, "was any of this fatal?" He saw it in his thoughts, "Skin would easily part for a bullet, like sand for a finger; once a finger is withdrawn from sand the grains roll back and fill in the hole as it was." From sand his thoughts moved to glass, "Of course when glass is broken it cannot not repair itself nor can it ever be fully restored—even by the most skillful glazier—unless it's melted and reformed (but even then is it ever the same glass?). But we are not glass. So how can a bullet kill a man? The bullet does not subtract from us even a single precious molecule.

"How can a bullet kill? What is housed in the body that it destroys?

"The soul? The soul is energy and energy cannot be destroyed."

The history slipped from his hand: the noise the book made when it hit the carpet was like a firm slap on Emile's back and brought him back to sense. To his more practical self. He knew again that bullets kill, and how, and that life is by its nature extinguishable.

"That is well documented," he said.

He leaned over, picked up the history.

"In this very book," he said.

He slid the book back into the space it had left on his desk. He took up his pen, put its tip to a blank notebook page, and began the tedious work of making.

His concentration on this work was not soothing but was forceful and good.

[PLATE 6]

"The Railway"

1873, 37¼ x 45

Bustle and billowing smoke. A blue bow as big as a girl. The woman looks up from her novel, leans a little to get a better look at us. If this were a film, the train would burst from the screen.

The au pair's charge, a little girl, holds onto the iron fence bars and watches the trains in the train station. Each weekday morning, commuters make a crowd, all through the turnstiles, all onto platforms. Wool suits and too many leather shoes. Each weekday morning, the au pair takes her charge to the station. Ostensibly, because the little girl likes to watch the trains, but actually, to look for the young man, who each weekday morning walks by, hurried, ever-late for something.

Steam rises and blows away, blows over the little girl and she squeezes her eyes shut and shouts, "The underground steam stacks!" The wind whines between the stopped trains: "And the underground whistle!" These are routine delights for the little girl.

After a morning visit to the trains nearly three weeks ago, an incidental stop on a long walk, the au pair remained ever-faithful to the young man. This attraction is indeed quite surprising, for the young man is fat and slovenly, a hand of hair fallen from his part, too-small suit jacket buttoned over his gut. Something about his face, maybe? Must be. His red hair matches the au pair's, though his is uncared for and hers is lovingly long and brushed.

On the au pair's lap is the little girl's dog, who must be walked. We must all be walked, thinks the au pair.

Of the trains, the little girl says, "They are like sleeping skyscrapers."

Every weekday, the au pair hopes the young man will see her. She certainly is stylish and she is pretty and she is not unsure about that. To no one in particular, and frequently, several days a week, the au pair says, "I will introduce myself." She hasn't. Her charge says, "If I turn my head to the side, the people inside are on their beds in their city apartments."

Apparently late again, a hurried gait and hurried expression on his face, the young man approaches the turnstiles, only a short distance from the au pair and her charge. The au pair makes an expression she imagines is both inviting and attractive (though she is not sure she is succeeding). The little girl, head still angled so the trains seem to stand on end, says, "They're rocket ships! They're rocket ships!" She's very excited by this.

Today, the clasps on the young man's briefcase pop open, and the contents of his case are dumped at the au pair's feet. The au pair is so surprised that the invisible fence between her and the young man is gone, removed by a stack of unbound papers, that she gives her charge's dog a squeeze. The dog yelps, and leaps from the au pair's lap. The young man rushes to gather his papers and says, "I'm so sorry," and, "I'm going to miss my train."

The au pair slides from the bench and kneels beside the young man. His face is red — from his hurry or does he blush? The au pair asks the young man his name and when he says, she whispers her own.

The little girl notices the young man for the first time and asks, "Do you ride the trains?" He nods his head, gathering pages.

The au pair, about to hand the young man a stack of his papers, sees that on the backs of the pages, written in pencil, are notes—not regarding the charts, but about her—at least, the mouth is right, the hair.

"Oh these are lovely," she says and, "I knew it!"

The little girl says, "You're an astronaut!"

And the young man? He is unsure.

[PLATE 7]

"Mlle. Victorine in the Costume of an Espada"
1863, 65 ½ x 50 ¾

Here, again, Goya lurks. Manet has yet to visit Spain, except by his romantic en-thusiasm for an exotic land. Victorine is posed with little regard for anything but a fine composition. The pink cape, as pink as nothing, floats away from the hand. A purple kerchief—not blue, as pink is not red—hides the hair of the girl posing as a man. A sword. A yellow cloth, the yellow of the pants of the picador pictured in the background.

I stand in the back of the theater and watch the man who comes to see the bullfight movie every day. The film has been in our second-run theater for a month, and from day one, he has come to watch. Our shows are cheap, and during the hot summer our theater is an air-conditioned escape for the underemployed. During weekdays, only two people are necessary to run the theater: the projectionist, who's union and so only rolls the film, and me, ticket seller, concession server, general manager. It sounds like a lot, but it's pretty low-key work.

I remember that the man came in for the very first show because he came dressed in full matador regalia, including a great wide-brimmed hat and—to taunt the bull—a small pink cape. On his hip, he wore a sword in a scabbard. I wasn't overly concerned. People who come to the theater during weekday afternoons are a little nuts. He pays for his ticket. If he wants to dress for the show, more power to him.

One of my jobs is to step into the theater during the shows and make sure the air-conditioning is good and that the projectionist hasn't fallen asleep and let the film glide out of focus. But honestly, the reason I religiously step into the bullfight film is to watch the man in the matador costume. I guess there isn't that much interest in a bullfighting documentary because there's never any audience other than us two.

There is a sequence in the film during which the bright white sand of the arena fills almost the whole screen. In the top corner, a section of the greenish wood wall is visible. During this sequence the man in the matador costume always rises from his chair and steps into the aisle. With this brilliant backdrop, he turns his right side to the screen and raises his pink cape. On the screen — in the movie — a man leads a picador across the arena. At this moment the man in the matador costume faces the screen: on-screen a bull appears. The bull faces us — the audience — then rushes toward us. Just as the bull seems to rush under the bottom edge of the screen, the man steps aside with a flourish of his cape. The scene changes then, and the man in the matador costume sits down. Always. Every day. And I can't see him do this often enough — his bullfight is so perfect, how he matches his actions with those of the film.

Today we're going to stop showing the bullfight film, and I'm anxious about it.

When the man in the matador costume buys his ticket for the last show, I look carefully at his face. A small, pale face, eyes bugged out, ears round and pronounced. I thought I'd mention to him that this was the last show, but when I see his determined expression — his trembling jaw — I stay quiet.

I stand in the back of the theater. As the scene approaches, I grow more excited, more and more now just moments before the scene. As the brilliant white sand appears, the matador man stands, bathed in the screen's white light. For the first time ever, he acknowledges that I'm there — he nods, this afternoon, to me. When the picador crosses the arena he tenses. But instead of raising his cape, he draws his sword. And when the bull appears on the screen, he charges.

[PLATE 8]

"The Balcony"

1869, 67 ³/₄ x 49 ¹/₄

This, though inspired by Goya's "Majas on a Balcony," buries Goya's sexual strains. The brunette with the piercing gaze is Berthe Morisot. Behind her is painter Antoine Guillemet. To the right is Jenny Claus, a violinist. That we see a skull of smoke above their heads is a wonder of paint chemistry and fear.

Berthe

Jenny and I sit on the balcony. Antoine, the best man, stands behind us. He looks like a bore but isn't so bad. Jenny *is* a bore except when she plays her violin. She saves her all for the violin. She sleeps nude with her violin. At least, that is how I have painted her today, as I aim my "gaze" across the lawn.

"Antoine, must you smoke such God-awful cigars?"

The clatter in the dining room is tedious. About a thousand dishes to be put away, and that's not hyperbole: the wedding is off. The big, fantastic wedding of Jenny's cousin is cancelled, so we won't dine on turtle soup, or gosling butter, or chicka-dee soufflé, or whatever other fashionable and cruel concoction the bride deemed *de rigueur.*

On the opposite end of the yard I see Francis begin his walk to Jenny's mansion, where I am, we are, where the wedding was to be held. Why, Francis, would you walk across Jenny's ridiculous backyard? And oh, Francis, everybody wants to be Jenny's violin, why must you also?

"Antoine, you're such a bore. Forget the groom."

Jenny's backyard contains no garden, no pool house, no hedge maze. Her backyard isn't even a simple flat of grass, available for family gatherings — thus, the wedding was to be held indoors. On such a fine day, too. Jenny's backyard is three high hills, hills smooth and round and grass-covered. Soon Francis will disappear behind the furthest hill — yup, gone — I can still see him, though. My gaze is famous.

Francis

There's a lot of speculation as to what the hills are (no one believes they're natural), speculation I don't contemplate as I polish off a cup of coffee, leave cup and saucer on my patio, and set out toward Jenny's. I wonder about getting over the three hills (a climb I regularly make) wearing patent leather shoes (and a pigeon-colored jacket, and vest, and striped trousers, and a striped tie with a pin in it). I could go the long way round, out the front, down the road, etc.; I could drive or be driven, but I'd prefer to go to Jenny's as I typically do: across my own yard, which *is* a flat of grass, just a flat plane of green green grass, to her yard (there is no fence between us), and over the three hills. I like this walk, shoes be damned.

Climb up the first hill (a little out of breath, unless I'm visiting Jenny often, and I mean, really, a lot). The second hill is higher than the first. From the first hill, only the roof of Jenny's mansion is visible, many-gabled, green-tiled. As I climb up to the top of the first hill I enjoy the illusion that I might take just a few steps further and be on Jenny's roof, where, I don't know, maybe I'd drop into her bedroom via the skylight over her bed. And then the hill slopes down to the shaded and narrow valley between the two hills.

(Sun up but not yet high, cool air, grass a little damp.)

(Jenny's backyard is three hills (the hill in the middle the highest). Three theories for three hills, three theories (with variations): buried beneath are bunkers, stocked in 1952; the hills are burial mounds with unnamed and ancient family members interred beneath; or that the hills are installation pieces by Robert Smithson, installed shortly before the plane crash that killed him.)

"I'd rather see a pile of dirt than a painting any day, wouldn't you?" Berthe likes to say (with a drawl that's put on).

That the hills are three massive unmarked graves is an idea for the morbid imagination only. I believe none of these stories. They are Jenny's hills and they keep the wedding I'm going to attend indoors, in the family chapel and then the ballroom, I suppose. The shadow the second (the highest) hill casts cuts across the ballroom floor. When I have guests (business), and am asked about the hills I repeat either the rumor that they are a Smithson installation or the rumor that they house bunkers, depending on my mood. The dead are bad for business.

Today, Jenny is a bridesmaid, as well as host, and will likely be pressed into playing violin during the reception. Likely pressed by *moi*.

The climb is difficult. I am careful to find purchase with each step, a trick in my patent leather. The first hill is easiest, its slope more gradual. In the valley between the two, it is very dark. And cool. My vest, which is silk, and my skin, which is pale, is green — reflects the grass that surrounds and immerses.

The grass on the hills can't be trimmed with mowers because the hills are too steep: several times a year the hills are peppered with men (wearing wide brimmed hats) who trim the grass with silver shears.

Berthe

The hills are not natural. Jenny's great-grandparents, or their parents, or *whatever*, built the hills. Whenever anyone asks me about the hills, I say, "I'd rather see a pile of dirt than a painting any day!" No one believes me. Sometimes the smell of turpentine makes me want to vomit. I heard that Jenny's grandparents intended to build follies atop each hill. The hills are follies all their own. Besides, the view is rotten. Mansions. A seagull occasionally settles onto our trash, blown in on some ill wind, but the sea is miles away.

"Look," Jenny says, "Antoine's puffed a perfect skull above his head."

I look. He has, in fact, and —

Francis' head emerges from the far side of the hill closest us: for a moment, he is only a head, his head bobs above the waving green — then shoulders, tie. He waves.

In spite of myself, I wave.

Francis

As I approach the top of the third hill, I'm at eye-level with the balcony, and the balcony looks as if it's set on top of the hill — a trick of this perspective. Berthe, Antoine, and Jenny are on the balcony. Antoine on his feet, cigar in hand; the ladies, seated. I'm confused. I expected they'd all be running around for the bride and groom, some nonsense. I pause on the hill and look at my watch. Still early, but in my experience, brides and grooms like to keep their entourage close at hand on the day of. I cup my hands around my mouth and shout: "Don't you all have work to do?" I expect someone (Berthe has the sharpest tongue) to shout back, perhaps to remind me that I've never done an honest day's work in my life ("'Tis true, 'tis true," I'm happy to admit).

Jenny speaks, but I can't hear what she says. Antoine hollers, "There's no wedding." I must *look* confused, and am — he hollers, "The wedding is off." Berthe shouts, "The wedding is cancelled!" and something else I don't understand. Behind the group, in the gloom of the ballroom, I see a man folding a tablecloth. Above Antoine's head is a cloud of smoke that makes the shape of an empty face.

I assume my friends are joking, so I shout, "What have you done to upset them?"

Berthe

Antoine points to the bolt with his cigar.

"I say," he says.

A bolt connecting the balcony to the house wriggles from its socket — a glimmer of oil. We do not leap from the balcony. I can't muster the panic to move. Jenny is hardly roused from her stupor.

"Indeed," Antoine says. Abruptly, he sits down — the seat of his chair cracks and Jenny jumps. I shout, "The wedding is cancelled because the groom . . . " Jenny stands and screams, "Shut up!"

Another bolt.

"Perhaps . . . " Antoine says, trying his level best to hold his chair together *and* to smoke his cigar.

Francis shouts a lame joke and loses his balance.

"He deserved that."

Francis tumbles back — but is caught by the hill — the balcony breaks free — we three are tossed against the green rail — staff inside the house shout and set to smashing dishes and stuffing prawns into their pockets. The wedding! I think. "My darling!" I shout.

Francis

When the balcony breaks loose from the house, it rises up, Antoine falls out of his chair to his knees — his chair — in pieces, flies off the back of the balcony, smashes to bits against the mansion — Antoine's cigar tumbles sparks, Berthe is thrown back, out of sight, and Jenny struggles to keep her balance, she's on all fours and she's screaming, to me, for help, or she's just screaming her confusion (her voice a violin). I tumble over backwards, but not down the hill, I'm carried on the crest of the hill — the sky, big, huge, empty, blue.

The hill carries me away from Jenny's house, the other hills rush around me, and the balcony rushes after me. Jenny is alone on the balcony — I catch glimpses as I swirl helplessly back toward my house, as I am engulfed in dirt and grass, as I try to keep my head up, clear — the sky. The hill moves like a wave but is hard like earth. Jenny reaches over the balcony rail — toward me? The balcony rolls forward and she disappears beneath. I yell: "These are waves!" I shout: "And graves!"

[PLATE 9]

"A Bar at the Folies-Bergère"

1881, 37³/₄ x 50

As quickly as he could, Manet put to canvas a scene glimpsed, including, even, his own image in a mirror, without any concern for composition. Instead, he rearranged what he saw in order to clarify what he felt, e.g., if the reflected girl is also the girl at the center of the picture, then Manet moved as he worked, thus bending hours into a single moment.

Behind the bar the mirror holds the memory of the night before. A crowd and their noise, glass and talk, and the bartender's back, and the conversation she had with the man who wore a top hat. This morning, the bartender stares. The sunlight encourages an easing, a relaxation of focus and mind, and her tiredness contributes. At her left hand, a cake dish piled with oranges.

The big window, through which she stares, is as big as the mirror behind her. The bar is terrible in the morning, but outside — on the brick of a building across the street, on the pale pavement, on the hairy-wood telephone poles, on the single, blue auto, and on the meter beside it — is sun, hours shy of its zenith. Soft sun. Light that begs to be lain in — she wishes, damp rag in her hand, saturating her palm till it's puffy and white. In the sunlight is goodness — ah! the oranges at her hand.

This sunny street scene includes no passersby. And then passes the man who wore the top hat, still dressed as if it were the night before. Indeed, the bartender notices, the flower he'd worn in his lapel the night before is there, wilted. He stands at the glass and smiles, just as he'd smiled the night before, and the bartender is compelled to ask, "What can I get for you?" though he is outside and cannot hear her. He says — she sees the words form and remembers how they sounded the night before — that he wants a club soda. Last night, she poured the drink. She watches as he says — as he'd said the night before — "I know a girl who is made of sand." She isn't sure she heard correctly. "Is that right," she says, as she'd said.

Through the window his mouth forms around the reply he'd given before: "Those are beautiful lilacs."

As part of her uniform, the bartender wears a cluster of lilacs pinned to her dress, just at the line of her cleavage. Men typically comment. His top hat gleams in the sun; she'd noticed the night before how the colored lights in the bar were reflected in the black silk. Men who comment on the flowers automatically receive poorer service, and she did not expect to say more to the man in the top hat, but now she knows that she did. He says, "I'm shipping out for another tour tomorrow."

There is sand, she thinks, where he might be shipped. Her cousin is in the war. All this, through the glass: the man who wears the top hat bathed in sun, his flower; she repeats her line, "I have a cousin in the Army." He repeats his line, "To your cousin, then," though she can still only see the words, cannot hear them. The bar is deeply quiet.

Club soda, an alcoholic's drink, she thought the night before, and again thinks how hard it must be, the night before deployment, in a lively bar, not to drink, and he mouths, through the glass, "I don't want to take advantage of you," and she grins as she'd done the night before, at the reversal that makes his joke funny.

Often, their conversation was interrupted by customers, and this morning, long pauses in their pantomime represents those interruptions. Whenever she'd had a moment, they talked, all night. She'd thought she might go home with him, and she'd worked up her line, something about his being tipsy and needing a ride, a little dumb but inviting, maybe even endearing.

The night before, he'd gone before she'd had the chance to use her line. This morning she brought to mind what she'd been about to say and—

A cloud moves in front of the sun and the scene outside the bar becomes dark, and the big window becomes a mirror. The bartender sees herself, and the empty bar, the bottles behind her, the plate of oranges. She watches herself pick up an orange.

And the sun lights the street again, and the man in the top hat is gone, again. A ghost, she supposes. Misery, she knows, lingers.

[PLATE 10]

"On the Beach"

1873, 20½ x 28⅜

A band of blue and five ships. A man and a woman on the beach. Her shoe is half buried beneath the sand of her dress while his hand, hidden from view, maps a course from shore to sea. A black ribbon, recalling Olympia's, is less like a noose, and more like a mourner's armband.

On the beach I was sure I saw a white kite float just above the sand, out to sea. A trick for the eye, played by the ocean and the moon. My boyfriend, on his back beside me, said, "I'll quit my job. I'll go out west with you." We were alone on the beach. We'd come to the beach to escape the heat and now I was a little cold. "Let me wear your shirt," I said. His shirt was crumpled beside him; he wore a t-shirt. I wasn't sure I wanted anyone to follow me out west. Clouds came together in front of the moon. "I can't see where the shore is," I said.

The shoreline crept, indistinguishable from the silver mud that preceded the water. Animals shuddered in the tall beach grasses. Kite shapes appeared to move toward us, and black shapes fizzled soda-static in the air above the unattended lifeguard towers. I moved close to my boyfriend, as if I wanted him to follow me out west. The clouds broke, and moonlight scattered across the ocean. He fell asleep. I did too.

I woke just prior to first light, to false light. The beach was misted gray light.

I startled at the sight of my boyfriend, asleep in a horrible position, the crown of his head pushed into the sand, his back arched up, hips turned, bare feet curled. His erect penis strained against his pants. I couldn't stand to see him so — I touched his stomach and instantly he relaxed and collapsed into the sand. He did not wake.

We were no longer alone. Another couple sat just beyond the lifeguard tower nearest to where we sat. On the beach, with so few landmarks, distance was hard to gauge. For a crazy moment, I thought the couple was right next to us. I said my boyfriend's name, and then wasn't sure I'd said it at all.

The man wore a rumpled coat and a beret; the woman a white dress and, drawn down over her face, a white veil. They faced the sea.

On a dark blue band of ocean, I saw ships.

Black shapes, growing, sails visible, then audible. The air was dead on the beach, but the ships' sails flapped rapidly, sails like kites. The ships were huge as they sailed into the shallows where the water was green. Surely the ships would ground soon. I stood. The man and woman stood. The massive ships sailed airily onto the beach. The ships cast whale-shadows. Where the boats were not, the air shone. Where they were was black, black.

The couple walked to the ships. He disappeared into their shadow; she was a white shape. She disintegrated.

The boats rose up and sailed backward. First from the beach, then out of the green shallows into the dark blue deep, over the lip of the horizon.

The beach shone bronze as first light broke for real.

I heard my boyfriend get up and pee.

Though the sun shone broad beams at me, I was as cold as I'd been when the woman had dissolved into the black ships, cold as the sky which was barely blue at all, as blue as ice sometimes is, as blue as pure white light.

"Claude Monet in His 'Studio'"

1874, 32 ¼ x 39 ⅜

Manet, Renoir, and Monet went together to paint at Argenteuil, where buoys ring as they bob back and forth. I was jealous I was not one of the boys. Manet's subject is Monet and his wife in the bark that Monet used as a summer studio. Light on water is Monet's.

She knows that the sea is hands. Hands slap the side of the boat. Hands lift the boat.

Claude is painting her. His subject is light.

I see this from the end of a dock. I see this: a man and a woman on a bark, safe from sun under a candy-striped cloth awning. His canvas glistens an oily gleam in the sun, his easel propped at the edge of the bark. His wicker sun hat, his beard. Her white dress a smudge of gray and peach. The water nearest the boat is dark blue; beyond the bark's shadow, crystalline.

She is not his muse. She is his source.

She talks while he paints. This keeps the nausea and ache at bay.

"I saw a hundred daffodils the other day."

Her voice carries over the water. I stop to listen and other passersby stop to listen. We watch. He paints and acknowledges what she says through his thick beard.

She says, "I wanted to trample those daffodils. Smash their yellow mouths against the grass."

He dips the tip of his brush into her skin, the pale skin of her throat, swirls the boar bristles around and again. His brush comes away water-blue. She moans, he winces. He paints with a delicate hand, making shape with color on his canvas.

We watch as a painting takes shape.

She says, "I hesitated only for the smallest moment. I rampaged through that patch of daffodils."

He swirls his brush in a glass of turpentine. Wisps of blue in a glass full of color. He wipes his brush on a cloth, dips the tip into her hand. The sound she makes is guttural, he turns away. The tip of his brush is purple. He attends to his painting.

There is a crowd behind me now; we watch, we listen from the dock.

She says, "All that was left was paste and mud and I felt good."

Hidden by his beard, his pale lips tremble.

He cleans his brush, looks at her. She owns all the light in the bay. She is a blur, she is oil-smoke.

He says, "You ought to take a dip."

She strips. Beneath her clothes, there is nothing for her to be modest about—there is nothing.

We who crowd the dock open our mouths, gasp. The dock sways, we sway. The number of onlookers has grown to a hundred.

Her shape dives into the bay. Oil keeps her skin dry. The water around her boils, fast, and is quick to cool.

He takes off his hat, wipes his brow.

When she pulls herself out of the water, back onto the bark, she is a whole woman. She shivers. He hands her a towel and she dashes into the cabin. He follows. He is through with paint for the day. The light has changed.

Hands pull at the dock. With so many people gathered there, I am certain the pilings will give.

We lean forward, to study the unfinished painting on the bark and to peer into the dark cabin. The dock tilts forward.

Paintings pile up on their boat, day upon day. The subject is light.

[PLATE 13]

"Blonde with Nude Bust"

1875, 31⅛ x 23¼

Here, Manet tests Impressionism. Here are the colors that came when he opened his studio to the charms of natural light. Bright, but not all: a green on the cusp of mildew, a somber ochre, and a blue that falls from the blonde's eyes to the hem of her thin chemise. His model's skin both rosy and blotched red."

My wife sat at the end of the guest bed in front of a Chinese cabinet. The doors of the cabinet were hinged in the middle; each panel, mirrored. At the back of the cabinet was another mirror. Her pale green dress on the bed: the remains of another her. She toyed with the strap of her slip as she stared at herself.

The elaborate braid of her hair drifted apart.

I poked around the room, stepped into dark corners, behind furniture, into closets.

"In a house like this," I said, "there could be hidden spaces." I caught my wife's faint smile in one of the cabinet mirrors. I caught her smile four times and saw it vanish, too. I loosened my tie and stepped inside a walk-in closet. Wire hangers jangled. I heard my wife say, "I thought the reception was lovely." I nodded agreement, though of course she couldn't see me. Whenever I spent the night in a strange place it was my habit to carefully examine the room. I looked into closets, drawers, vents, and knotholes. I looked behind wall-mirrors and framed prints. I checked under the bed. This bordered on ritual, this searching for hidden spaces. I wanted to occupy the whole room.

In the back of the closet was a hatbox. As I pulled the box down, dust curled off the shelf, rained over me. I carried the box into the room and said, "Look at this." The box was pale blue.

My wife looked at me in one of the mirrors. "What is it?" she asked.

Her slip was in a pile around her hips; her bra was on the bed beside her. In the mirrors, I stood around her, four of me proffering a pale blue box.

I opened the box. "I don't know. It looks like a big yellow slipper."

She said, "Bring it here." She took the dusty box from me. I sneezed. She said, "God bless." I looked at her breasts in a mirror. As I stared at her breasts, I watched my hand in a mirror, in another, as I reached forward to touch her shoulder.

"It's a hat," she said. She turned at the waist and put on the hat. I undid the knot of my tie. "It's ridiculous!" she said. "I wonder whose it was?"

"Your aunt's?"

My wife didn't reply. She stared at the flat mirror at the back of the cabinet. She leaned forward. "I wonder if my aunt ever used this cabinet. It's like a magician's box. It makes me sleepy." She took off the hat and stood up. I saw her lower back, her bottom, in the mirror. Her slip fell to her feet. She said, "Honey, I'm pregnant." She patted her belly, flat, yet. She closed the cabinet doors; the cabinet was transformed into a wooden box.

That my wife was pregnant was not news. We'd known for weeks.

My wife said, "You have the biggest, silliest grin on your face."

In the morning, while my wife was still asleep, I picked up the yellow hat from the floor. I stood in the middle of our guest room, dressed only in boxer shorts (band stretched around my ample waist). The weekend was going very nicely. My wife's favorite cousin had been married. My wife and I had danced together. And, arcing over all those little details, we were going to have a child. I opened the mirror-cabinet. My face, flat, repeated.

"Luncheon in the Studio"

1868, 47 ¼ x 69

All the objects in the studio shine: glass, porcelain, metal, oysters, glass, the oily sur-
face of a lemon, pale blue china, lead, and velvet. It is that all the objects shine:
though static a still life may be, each piece speaks movement.

My publishers were in their dining room; I'd come on appointment, found the front
door to their house open and followed the sounds of rattling glasses. I was there to
discuss what next to do with my manuscript, which they'd accepted three years ago,
which I'd been steadily revising and expanding to their specification.

Framed by a set of double doors: the elder publisher and the younger, a long table
covered by a white tablecloth, to the left of the table a red chair. Piled on the chair
were pieces of armor and two swords, one with a curved blade, the other a golden
grip. The elder publisher sat behind the table, smoked a pipe and stared off past the
red chair. The younger publisher, dressed in yellow pants, a black velvet jacket, and a
yellow hat, stood in front of the table, hand in pocket.

"Good. You found us," he said.

I said, "The door was open."

On the table was a plate of oysters over ice, a lemon—curl of peel dangled—a wine goblet, and a tea cup.

A woman walked into the room, dressed like an English chambermaid and carrying a teapot on a silver tray. She looked at me, said, "Anyone for gin?" The elder publisher tapped his tea cup. A black cat leapt from the floor to the red chair; the armor sounded like tin cups close together in a cupboard. The woman poured gin from the teapot—for the elder publisher and for herself—and lit a cigarette.

I was about to ask if a spot could be found on the table for my manuscript when the young publisher said to me, "You're a mind. I've been saying a man's only free before he's made commitments. What do you think?"

"Well—of course," I said. Because—of course.

"No. I mean, when a man's still young. When he's still at home, living with his parents, going to high school, imaging what his life will be. Once you go to college—because there he thinks he'll be free—once he buys a car to be free, once he meets a beautiful woman . . . then he's no longer free."

"What you've said," the woman said, "is that desire precludes freedom."

"I don't think that's what I've said," the young publisher said. "A man's freedom is in the mind. Once a mind cannot conceive of another life—" He looked at me—"You see?"

I said, "That sounds good." The elder publisher put down his pipe and slurped up an oyster. I didn't wish to be controversial with my publishers. I looked for a clear spot on the table to put down my manuscript—my arms were tired. Though, I wished also to maintain poise—this was the meeting that would see my manuscript published, all the hoops these men had asked me to jump through, accomplished.

The woman shook her head, ate an oyster, drank some gin.

The cat flicked its tail against the helmet on the red chair, curled its tail around the curved sword-blade.

"People think, now that I'm married," said the young publisher, "that I'm no longer free. But from such stability, new possibilities arise."

I thought that once my manuscript was published I would have such stability.

"Certainly you agree," the young publisher said. Before I could speak he said, "And they're free? Every weekend the same. Every weeknight the same. They think to dingle a different woman — no offense — " the young publisher said.

The woman grunted.

The young publisher said, "They think that's freedom. With all that terror and desperation, how can they be free?"

I wasn't sure who they were but I nodded. My manuscript was enormous. I tried to find a way to step around the young publisher to put my manuscript down on the table. The young publisher leaned over and picked up the helmet from the red chair. The cat leapt to the table and dipped its tongue into an oyster shell.

"Why have we got this?" the young publisher asked. He put the helmet on over his yellow hat.

The woman said, "For protection."

I put my manuscript down on the table. The cat jumped up onto my manuscript and stood on it. The elder publisher looked at me. I smiled. He said, "We're not taking your manuscript after all. No one is interested in ideas anymore. Your manuscript is unpublishable."

At first I stood stunned; stress piled onto my shoulders. Rage came quickly; I took the sword with the gold grip and swung it at the young publisher. The sword crashed into his helmet. The young publisher fell over onto the red chair, knocking over the curved sword and the rest of the armor.

The elder publisher said, "But do, do try elsewhere."

I could've smote them all — that gold-gripped sword could've halved the cat and my manuscript with a single blow.

[PLATE 16]

"The Fifer Boy"

1866, 38½ x 23½

Remove the fifer boy, and the canvas is left with the tune; remove the background, and the fifer is left naked. Naked as the model Victorine was in "Luncheon on the Grass," in "Olympia," or when her body was prepared for her wake. Here, flat tones rather than careful grading. Here, shadows cast on nothing.

After the memorial service, the nephew retreated from his family to his aunt's attic. With the trap down, he could just hear the hum of those below. The nephew had found the service to be inadequate.

In the attic, set in front of a cloth hung from a beam (a cloth once white but now gray with mildew), was the sewing dummy, still dressed in the band uniform jacket and cap that'd been on it for as long as the nephew knew about the dummy. Beneath it was a circle of shadow cast from the coat.

The nephew sat before it with his legs folded. In his head, he concocted a prayer, of sorts.

He heard the ladder steps creak and turned to see who would emerge from the open rectangle in the floor.

"I thought I'd find you here," his fiancée said. "What's going on?"

"When I was a boy I used to come up here a lot. I always wanted to wear that jacket, but it was forbidden."

The nephew's fiancée sat beside him. When he walked around in the attic, he hunched over to avoid hitting his head. His fiancée cleared the low beams without bending.

"It's a lovely coat," she said. She reached for it, but retracted her hand before she touched it.

"It was my great-grandfather's when he was a boy. He played the fife. See—" He tapped a brass case which hung at the jacket waist. Inside the case he heard the instrument move.

"I was having a funny kind of memory before you came up." He rested his hand on her leg. She wore a black skirt, stretched taut across her lap.

"What's that?" she asked.

"When I was twelve I was up here looking at this coat, fantasizing, having fun, when I suddenly became sad. I thought, when my aunt dies, this will remind me of her more than anything else."

"That's a dark thought for a boy to have."

"That's probably why I remember having it."

"Maybe you can have the coat."

"It belongs up here."

She leaned against him. He put an arm around her.

"I wasn't just thinking about that. Our aunt let us have so much fun when my sister and I were kids. She'd babysit. She let my sister ride her bike in the house on rainy days. She let my sister eat cereal from a bowl set on the floor."

"Why did your sister want to do that?"

"So she could pretend to be a dog."

His fiancée laughed. He felt good.

"I told my aunt that Mom made us plain jelly sandwiches — no peanut butter — and my aunt made them for us. She knew what was going on, but boy did we think we were getting away with murder."

He kissed the top of his fiancée's head. "Why don't you put the coat on?" he said.

"No."

"It's too small for me. I could've worn it as a boy, but it's too small now. But you're small."

"You really want me to?"

"Yes. That would be perfect."

She put on the jacket. She slipped the strap of the fife case over her head. She removed the fife, brought it to her mouth and blew out a few bright notes.

The fabric of the coat cracked like ice on a puddle.

[PLATE 17]

"The Execution of Emperor Maximilian"

1867, 96½ x 118⅛

Goya lurked. Cut this execution to pieces.

This story happened before television ceased to be.

When I was twelve I found a television set in the woods. A small black and white set with a handle on the top and a screen curved and thick like a magnifying glass. During the day, I kept the set under my bed.

My bedtime was nine. I learned to wait, awake, listening closely to my parents: the fly buzz of their conversation, dishes, their footsteps. I heard the house, too. The house twisted and its bones clicked and groaned. When my parents went upstairs, I'd set the television at the end of my bed and watch. Only two channels. The local channel broadcast its own peculiar shows at night. The later the hour, the more peculiar—and most peculiar as night crossed over into morning. Thus, I saw the first midnights I remember. I kept the volume to a whisper and when shows were really scary I turned the volume all the way down. I never stopped watching.

I watched the show "The Execution" that way: black and white television at the foot of my bed, room dark and house twisting, volume off. A storm interfered with the reception. The title, "The Execution," in white letters. The picture formed as the words disappeared. A forest with white trees. The camera panned a complete circle so I saw as if I stood in the woods and slowly turned completely around. A stone wall rose like steps. Three men, holding hands, one dressed in a black suit, with a big hat and a ribbon pinned to his coat. Five soldiers, their guns up and aimed at the three men. Another soldier behind the five, inspecting his gun. At the top of the wall were a group of children looking down upon the scene. The camera kept moving. Before the three men slipped off the left edge of the television screen, smoke appeared over the five soldiers' guns and the three men fell over. The soldiers who'd fired lowered their guns and stepped aside for the soldier who'd stood behind them. This sole soldier walked toward the three men. The camera moving all the while — the three dead men were no longer on screen and soon the sole soldier was also off-screen. I turned on the volume — there was nothing to hear. Soon the camera's eye reached the end of the wall, then panned beyond the end of the wall. I stared into the white forest as it dissolved to colorless static.

One afternoon I went off one of the trails, sure I could cut to a parallel trail. I beat my way through briars and branches. I followed a stream. I saw a black dirt hill and climbed it to see where I was. The hill rose to the top of a stone wall. When I looked down, I saw a soldier checking his rifle, I saw five soldiers with their guns up, aimed at three men, I saw three men, holding hands. The man in the middle was dressed in black with a big hat and a brilliant red ribbon. I stood until the five soldiers fired. The sound must have been massive, but I can remember no sound at all, just the sight of oily smoke rising from their guns.

I ran down the hill, toward the path I'd left. I heard — I stumbled when I heard — a single gunshot.

I didn't tell anyone about what I'd seen. I didn't watch television that night. I listened to the house and I imagined a great pair of hands twisting the house: God's hands.

When I was twelve I was in the woods following a path I hadn't been down yet, the path I'd chosen not to take again and again.

That path opened to a circle of white trees. At the center of this coppice was a shed without a door. I dared myself, and dared myself, and finally looked into the shed. In the shed was a long wooden table. On the table were three boxes. They were small; no larger than the television I'd found. I stepped into the shed—I smelled mildew, earth, a whiff of something else, sharp, sweet, smoky. I looked into the first box. I saw toy soldiers—five—pointing rifles at three toy men, hands clasped, one dressed in a black suit with a big hat and a red ribbon on his lapel. Behind the five soldiers, I saw a sixth, checking his gun. The box was a wall that went all around the scene. In the second box I saw five toy soldiers, parted, a single toy soldier among them, three toy men on their backs, arms thrown up over their heads. In the third box I saw five toy soldiers standing with their backs to a single soldier, his gun pointed at a smear of red paint, where the head of the toy man in the black suit should have been. A big hat a few inches from the three toy men on their backs. The red ribbon on the toy man without a head undone.

I walked around the table.

I reached into the first box and picked up the toy soldier who stood checking his gun. I held his chest between my right thumb and index finger, his legs between my left thumb and index finger. I twisted the toy soldier—his soft lead body gave, tore apart like a piece of taffy. The sound it made when torn apart was like little thunder. In this museum, I was giant.

All this happened before I turned thirteen. All this happened when there was still television.

[PLATE 18]

"Boating at Argenteuil"

1874, 58⅝ x 44⅛

Bright sun caught swirling in the clouds overhead and in the blue waters at Argenteuil. Everything is in flux. Touches of the brush deposit little glints of light on multiple surfaces. Lines cross.

A woman and a man are on a boat. The boat is anchored in a bay. The man thinks the day is a special day. They are brightly dressed. The air is salt sweet.

The woman says, without looking at the man, "Picture: three boys leap from a dock, a twelve-foot jump to the water below. Jump one after the other. Dark-haired boys with dark skin all wearing blue shorts. In the air, one leg up, the other back; a groundless run. Three splashes.

"One boy emerges from the water, the second, the third. But—then a fourth boy emerges, a fifth, a sixth and so on. Dark-haired boys emerge all around the dock, pop up, boys pop up further and further from the dock—dozens, hundreds, thousands. Boys fill the bay, bare shoulders gleam in the sun. An ocean of boys, bobbing like plastic bath toys, rocking gently against each other, soundless, stiff. The horizon—once the glassy eye-curve of the ocean—now row upon row of boys.

"The land is land. Beach. Red-tan sand that ripples out of sight. Further inland, tall green grasses, houses.

"How can there be boating, if to sail would be murder? No one can leave this island surrounded by boys. And what do the fishermen expect? That their nets won't come up heavy with boys? Even clam-diggers must be careful they don't chop off an arm with their spade."

That's the picture the woman makes for the man. He looks at her. She stares ahead, at the sea, blue and clear, at the sky with white and gray mottled clouds like a pigeon's egg. The man holds her folded parasol across his lap. He fiddles with its mechanism. That evening, he plans to take her to a restaurant on the island. The woman's face betrays amused contemplation: she sees her horror of boys, not the busy waterfront. She suspects that later the man will ask her to marry him.

She says, "Picture: three boys. They jump from a dock. As they fall, their thick hair stands like black flames atop their heads. Three splashes. Trails of bubbles. One boy emerges from the water, and then the second boy. But—no third boy breaks the surface. The two boys swim, climb the dock ladder and jump, swim, climb the dock ladder and jump; those two boys repeat themselves all morning. When the sun is at its highest, the two boys go home for lunch. They leave the bay as if there never had been a third boy. The island goes on as if there had never been a third boy.

"The ocean is a desert and when scorched it becomes glass. Beneath the ocean are animals and plants born in the water. Among them and ignored by them stands detritus from the rest of the world."

The woman has already decided. If the man asks her to marry him she will say no. She could tell him stories for the rest of her life but she does not love him. That is as plain as the wood deck beneath their feet. The woman says, "When fishermen net the third boy, they know that the only thing to do is to chop him up for chum. They know to do this is right, because he is not true."

[PLATE 19]

"White Lilacs and Roses"

1883, 22 x 18

With Victorine dead, there was little Manet wished to paint. This picture's life comes not from the flowers, which can only be fooled for so long by water and sunlight, but from the master's brushwork: quick application, short strokes. I see a still life.

His ability to find regret. Memories are sifted through, the silt being what is everyday, one thousand unmemorable bus rides, pleasantries exchanged with people who find you of little interest, vice-versa, etc., etc. Amid this silt are minerals with weight. Polished and cut, they become a glowing focus.

An aimless afternoon during the early days of spring, when a heavy coat was as likely carried as worn, our man ran into Alison. Alison and our man knew each other from school, both at least a year and a half from their degrees. Alison was always friendly, which confused our man as much as anything, since he lacked the confidence to believe someone as lovely and, in fact, gorgeous as Alison could possibly have "the time of day," etc., for him. She did, as we have guessed, not only have time for our man, but harbored a crush, for he was lanky, awkward, kind, well-mannered, and a reader. Not like the boys in Newton, North Carolina. Our man knew which fork to use, which spoon, when, where, and that there was a difference. Which mattered to Alison. All this, true, though our man thought very little of his accomplishments, and worried he was not enough like the clever men Alison seemed to him to prefer.

She asked, Where are you going?

He said, To the movies.

Until that moment, he hadn't thought at all about where he was going, and was as surprised as we are that he answered so assuredly.

However, no more surprised than our man was when Alison asked, May I join you? She neither knew what movie he planned to see nor cared; good, since our man neither knew nor cared either.

Sure, he said.

Serendipity took over: a leisurely ride by subway to the theater that showed, for two dollars a ticket, second-run films; a film starting in (a glance at his watch) just a few moments; and a classic he'd never seen but was her professed favorite.

No arm around her shoulder, not a hand on her knee, but, finally, exasperated, Alison rested her head on our man's shoulder. He did not move an inch. His joy was expressed by rigid, "nervous tension." He had not the slightest idea how the characters in the film had reached Paris.

After the movie, Alison took our man to a wine shop, where she purchased a very young red. As she waited to pay, as she paid, as the clerk bagged her bottle, our man was wide-eyed and silent: maybe, maybe he could pass for twenty one, but Alison? No, she looked nineteen, looked as young as seventeen (though, he admitted, when she spoke she spoke like a woman civilized in, oh, he didn't know, London, maybe).

I was almost out of wine, she told him, as they left the shop.

Wow, he said.

She lived in a dormitory, in "a single." She tucked the bottle in her sweater; she'd done so before. Our man thought, This went so well. Alison said, You can come up with me. Our man, afraid he might mess up a perfect afternoon, unsure just what he would say to Alison in her room, said, That's alright. I should go. A moment, dumb, without motion. They parted ways without so much as a peck on the cheek.

The glowing focus, the regret that he did not go up to her room, opens a door, only slightly, but, a decade and more out of college, a divorce inevitable, a pessimism so deep it splinters his bones, our man slips through the open door. He stands in front of Alison's dormitory. Surprising, perhaps, but also, not a surprise.

Much did happen between Alison and our man in the years following that fine and regrettable afternoon. They did see each other, kisses and more snuck away from other lovers, and late night, pleading phone calls. Less dramatic moments, too, sitting side-by-side on a porch, glasses of wine, catching up, wondering, Why don't we spend more time together? The timing was always bad, or one was oblivious to the other.

He enters the building. The doors are unlocked. The front desk is unmanned. No students occupy the halls or the elevator. He rides to her floor, walks to her room. He never saw her room, but here, in this place, he knows exactly where she is. He opens the door. Alison is there. She is perfectly still. She is a glass vase, overflowing with white lilacs and roses.

book two
EDGAR DEGAS

[PLATE 20]

"Head of a Young Woman"

1867, 10 ⅝ x 8 ⅝

Of American women, Degas said they all were pretty, and that "amidst their charms, that touch of ugliness without which, no salvation." Her red hair may have been red, though the brush dipped in the red of her lips suggests otherwise. Her mouth. Her eyes. When I look long enough, I see the great bruise undercoat.

She is my wife does she know I lust after her?

Even in college I knew to say all women are beautiful — yes, even those who aren't, they are: those women with beautiful weight, beautiful mucked-up faces. Grotesque women. Women aren't grotesque. All women are exquisite and cause a band of ache across my abdomen, a tension that compels me to look, look, look. This isn't ogling. Ever see a man turn around to get a glimpse of a woman's ass? *He's* crude. I do not find women in bathing suits any more exciting than women in knee-length skirts and wool jackets.

My wife is on the other side of the gallery. The wall behind her is green. A black shirt with a collar, dark jeans. Her red hair is held back with a black ribbon. My wife has a large nose — bulbous, even; below it a dainty mouth.

I watch her look at a painting and I want to undress her. I'd like to step into a shower with her and stand behind her, my erection pressed to my stomach by her buttocks, the head of my penis against the small of her back. She is petite. I am larger. I've gone soft in the gut. I would twist my finger in her pubic hair. I would, and with my hand I'd cup her belly, soft but small, my index finger dipped in and out of her shallow belly button. We, damp, sheet: yes, I look at other women — but not now, now my lust for my wife holds my attention. I am *checking her out*. I am *getting an eyeful*.

Yesterday, there was the woman in the khaki skirt. We talked about tennis, then accounting, then the city we'd both once lived in. She offered me her phone number. Perhaps a tennis match? The day before yesterday, there was the woman who wore the blouse that accentuated her great breasts, breasts larger than I've ever held — she and I never spoke but exchanged glances in a hotel lobby. My good friend Louis believes in infidelity, must consume all the women he can. I do not share his need. I do not project other women onto my wife; though, undoubtedly, other women are layered into me and expelled sheet by sheet every time my wife and I make love, talk, eat cereal together, clean our apartment.

My wife's beauty is complex and ever-revealing.

When alone with my wife, I barely know what to do with her.

My wife lies on her back after we've made love. She pictures a glass jar, a large jar, the size of a newborn. She pictures the jar emerging from her ribs, just below her breasts. A ring of glass, open, ridges for a lid. The body of the jar, a curve, a column. The thick glass bottom, stippled. The jar is filled with tension, a little bit of the future, a bit of her past (perhaps).

The jar rises from her body, floats up, floats up through the ceiling, out of our apartment, out through the roof of the building, blazes through the atmosphere. The jar is in outer space.

I am beside her in bed. I cannot send a jar into space because I cannot give birth. Not all women can give birth, but no man can. My wife's beauty reveals itself. Is layered into me.

[PLATE 21]

"Spartan Girls and Boys Exercising"
1860, 42⅞ x 61

History was all too often stiffly reproduced by the French Academy and by cameras. Degas remembered more vividly. The young men stand about, maybe stretch, but the young women embrace each other and the air. The air is a million colors.

One final performance of the high school play. My role was small but opposite the girl whose seat was in front of mine during algebra class. She was casual with her homework. She carried a purse that brimmed with tobacco. Her heart wasn't in math or theater. I was attracted to her lack of passion. A lack paired with natural talent. Our lines were as follows:

HER: Are you going to the cast party?

ME: Yeah. You are too, right?

HER: Sure. There's gonna be beer.

ME: Great.

HER:

ME: I don't mean to, you know, I wouldn't want—

HER: You need a ride.

ME: Yeah. Is there room in your car?

HER: You'll have to clear off the front seat.

ME: OK.

HER: So when we're done—

ME: Yeah. I know your car. What lot are you parked in?

HER: The graveyard lot.

ME: OK. I'll meet you at your car.

ME exit stage left. HER exit stage right. The play ends and they meet in the graveyard lot. She is smoking a cigarette. Cue oily clouds over the full moon. Cue wind. Cue air. Cue the smell of red licorice.

I was thrilled to be in her car. I loved her every day of the week.

Though she gave me rides in her car, and let me copy her homework, I couldn't be sure if she liked me at all. With her, there was no being sure of anything. The radio was playing a popular song. I asked her if she liked the song. She shrugged and said, "You can change it, if you want." I hadn't thought that far ahead.

I had thought about being her boyfriend. I was sure I'd be a good boyfriend, because I would be devoted to her, endlessly. I knew this. The shape of the knot of hair on the top of her head led me to that discovery: by following the course of her hair, its faulty spiral, I found that love gathered in the dark center of her head. Her brain that sat in cooled liquid.

She drove and we tried to follow the directions we'd been given. Her car smelled like McDonald's French fries and tobacco. These were heavenly smells. Her face was caked in stage makeup, but the back of her neck was bare. Light wavered along her spine, down the back of her blouse.

"I'm cold," she said. She upped the temperature. I was sure I'd die in the heat. But in her car. With her.

I watched her hand on the stick shift. I looked at the bare knee closest me. In her small car, very close to me.

We drove to the end of the pen-drawn map.

"We're lost," she said.

"I know," I said. I was in heaven. We could wander in her car all night and I'd be glad.

We were on back roads. My job was to look for Lycurgus Street.

"It should be on our right."

Another popular song. There were so many popular songs on the radio in those days.

I tried to imagine the act of proposing love to her. I could imagine what my life would be like after I proposed love and she agreed to my proposal. We would kiss (cue her lips; they were small, thin, pale pink). We would talk about God and art. Art and God. Art, art, art. Her teeth were bright though she smoked. I could also imagine what my life would be like after I proposed love and she said no, no, I'm not in love. I would plummet into infinite depths of sorrow.

But I could not imagine proposing love. Not in a clear, realistic way. The words involved wouldn't come in. Not like words in a script. Not typed in black on white. Written, instead, on wax paper with a white grease pencil and smudged by my own clumsy hand.

I saw the street and so did she.

We turned right.

We were an hour late and there were rumors about us that excited me. I studied her face for clues but her expression was shadowed by flame from her lighter. The party was in the basement. The parents would rather us drunk in their basement, than drunk elsewhere. The music was too loud. Who knew so many of us smoked. Who knew? The light was bad. Girls and boys danced and made out and talked.

Our hostess, the star of the play, popular, voluptuous, said, "Let's go to the pond and skinny dip!"

That it was fall was pointed out. But a group, three girls and four boys, were eager to go.

And *she* said she would go, her, so I went.

There wasn't any light at the pond. The clouds had covered the moon. I'd never seen a girl naked before. I'd never been naked in front of a girl. In the face of this happening, I couldn't imagine taking off my clothes but I took off my clothes. Was I attractive? I wanted to see her naked without looking. I didn't want anyone else to see her naked.

We didn't run for the water. The star of the play, so much more voluptuous than I could have guessed, delivered to five naked boys (myself included) the first line of the play. One of the boys fell on all fours. He'd played the dog. He was looking between the legs of a girl not yet fully undressed — topless — but still wearing her black skirt.

I thought we should get into the water as quickly as possible. Where was the pond? Lines were delivered back and forth.

She was naked and huddled close beside another naked girl. Whose legs were those?

A crowd from the party, all dressed in their costumes, gathered in the distance to see us naked. When our scene came, she stepped forward and addressed me. Our lines were as follows:

HER: Are you going to the cast party?

ME: I feel sick every time I see you.

HER: Sure. There's gonna be beer.

ME: You're the most beautiful girl I've ever seen!

HER:

ME: I've sketched the whorl of your hair in the margins of my notes every day since I met you.

HER: You need a ride.

ME: When I hear a song on the radio and they're singing about love, I know what they mean!

HER: You'll have to clear off the front seat.

ME: I've never understood anything. The light you cast —

Cue the wind. The clouds move and reveal the moon. HER nakedness is vivid white. ME is trembling. ME and HER face each other. HER reaches forward and touches his chest. HER touches his chin. HER brushes his thigh with the back of her hand. ME lets out a yell. Cue thunder (backstage a tin sheet is shaken). HER takes his hand in her own and guides it toward her belly. The boys and girls and the costumed partygoers in the background form a half-circle around HER and ME.

CHORUS: (a song about tall grasses and a pond that looks like a smudged thumbprint).

HER: So when we're done —

ME: Yeah. I know your car. What lot are you parked in?

HER: The graveyard lot.

ME: OK. I'll meet you at your car.

HER: The graveyard lot.

ME: Life is revealing.

[PLATE 22]

"The Dancing Class"

1876, 32⅝ x 29⅞

Here, Degas cut one figure with another. He overlapped their forms masterfully; figure and form so shrewdly fit together there is not confusion but depth. We reach in with our hands. Where there are no dancers, there are our hands.

The inside of her father's spacious shoebox was green like the walls in her dance studio. She hadn't been to ballet class in two months. Her legs were broken: in two places, in three. Two weeks ago, she had discovered shadowboxes.

That's what they were called. Shadow. Boxes. Little theaters to stage frozen dances. To see a place: inside a box. To see a place in miniature.

The shadowboxes she had made topped the low shelf beside her bed. When on her back, she could turn her head and look into her shadowboxes. The nurse said, "If you stare into those boxes long enough, little lady, you'll shrink." That had happened once, just before the girl fell asleep. The girl knew dreams were dangerous.

The girl spent her days in bed. Her father had provided her with a lap easel for a firm surface on which she could cut and glue. The first shadowbox she made was sloppy, to her mind. She could now glue and cut with grace and technical sweep. She no longer sketched her figures before she cut them out: she cut the shapes of girls and boys and monsters freehand from blank Bristol board, cut them so they kissed and climbed, and so they devoured.

She was allowed to use the sharpest pair of scissors. She hid the drops of blood that fell on her cut-out figures with crayon and watercolor.

With black paper she built a set of bleachers, and with black and brown paper she cut four mothers to watch over dance practice. With red tissue paper she cut a scarf, with green, a hat. The mothers sat with arms crossed. Her own mother wasn't in that shadowbox.

For her mother, the girl imagined another shadowbox, a car shadowbox, driving away. The girl's mother wondered: "Now that my girl will never dance again, can she be free to do as she pleases?" The thought came and went like a cup of coffee in a car's cup-holder.

The girl cut fourteen little ballerinas. She cut a mirror from white paper—the way white paper caught color was like a mirror, the girl thought. With watercolor, she dabbed peach and pink on the ballerinas: a bow, a flower. She cut an instructor, an old man with a cane. The girl missed the instructor: she cut him from a sheet of bright yellow.

Her instructor once came by the house to visit his "wounded swan." He brought her a little book with reproductions of paintings in it. He'd said, "Many of these paintings are of dancers. I hope that won't make you sad. I hope you'll see and realize that there are many ways to dance."

He'd given her a pat on the head, and when the nurse wasn't looking, a chocolate "filled with elixir." The chocolate made her warm like tea going down, but thick and sweet.

The girl arranged the paper ballerinas: they warm up before class, they chit-chat. She had liked to chit-chat, but she couldn't remember what she'd chit-chatted about any-more. She cut the legs off the last paper ballerina and kept her outside the shadowbox.

The girl made a shadowbox for her father. She painted the inside of the box black.

She made a brown paper table and a gray paper father. He rested his head on the table-top and fell asleep.

Her father came up to visit her at night, when he thought she slept. He said, each night, "God bless you. God bless you."

The girl understood her life was miniature. Her room, her house, her country, her planet. In space, the stars hung on invisible wire. She asked herself, when she couldn't sleep, "Is there another me?"

The most dangerous dream the girl had ever had: she'd been dancing on air. She'd felt as if there was nothing to hold her back, that the world was vast and open. Her feet moved perfectly, as she wished they would move in class. She was full of joy.

When she woke from that dream, she fell from the roof of her house.

[PLATE 23]

"The Dancing Class"

1880, 24 ¾ x 18 ⅞

Where the ballerinas and the mothers are not is yellow. The wood floor swirls under shadow, light, and chalk. White ribbons shine at the girls' throats, at their waists, are threaded through their hair. I, too, am entangled, with Degas, his paint.

The hours in the classroom: his daughter's enviable energy. When she sleeps, she plummets. Her cheeks, they flush, and she becomes still, sinking into her mattress so deeply he's afraid he'll lose her.

Wavering like paper at the kitchen table, he has a glass of milk by his left hand. The kitchen is dark save the light from the moon that comes in through the little window above the sink. The moonlight is whiter than milk; water-white. The trees are luminescent. Their home — his and his daughter's — is surrounded by luminescent trees. Not just birch, so obviously luminescent, but Engelmann, juniper, and Ponderosa pine.

He is the only father observing the dancing class. The women, the mothers, first attend to their daughters. They adjust the girls' slippers, ribbons, and the gauzy costumes that are cute on the littlest girls, too revealing on the girls a little less little. The women, there to watch, seem to know that the father's wife is gone. That his wife packed up the good car and drove to her new apartment, keeping secret wishes for her daughter and her husband. The women seem to know that the father sits at the kitchen table stiff like a paper doll, contemplating cold light. After they attend to their daughters, they attend to him: they've brought a cup of coffee, "I can't finish this bagel, would you like it?" they surround him on the bench where he sits to observe his daughter dance. The women wear brand-new workout suits. The little dancers move from one end of the studio to the other.

During an afternoon class, his daughter fell. She was so light the sound she made as she hit the wood floor was only air pushed abruptly aside. His daughter's teacher, seeing that she was all right, accused her of sleep-dancing. The girls giggled. A woman in a black workout suit, the woman who couldn't finish her bagel, took the father's hand in her own and squeezed: two lines that fell from the corner of the woman's mouth made her look sad though she smiled.

The sun comes into the dance class brilliantly; the green walls go yellow.

When his daughter fell he stood a little — butt and thighs off the bench, legs rope-taut and tense. When his daughter leapt to her feet as quick as light as light as air his muscles relaxed and he settled back onto the bench; he found his hand in the hand of a woman in a black workout suit.

While seated at his kitchen table, the father walks through the woman's house. He can't remember her exactly, a peripheral being, a black spot bouncing in his vision, taking him through her house. Her house is small. The rooms are neat. Look at the living room; it's round. The light isn't very good and the bookshelves are only decorated with books, the books people end up with. Look down the hall: a painting of rippling water — there's a story behind that — a small table with a porcelain cup. Look in my daughter's bedroom, she's at school, won't be home for a few hours. Look into my bedroom, go on ahead, see, there's another painting of rippling water — there's a story behind that. The father asks for coffee, pushes his way out of the bedroom, he wants to see the neighborhood, he can't tell if the woman is frowning or if it's just the lines drawn from the corners of her mouth. While at his kitchen table he walks through that woman's house imagining that he lived there, that her daughter was his own, that he's come across the same painting of rippling water twice in the same month, hundreds of miles apart. He feels his body fold.

Outside, a sound like snow falling from high branches and he hears his daughter cry out. The kitchen table is shoved back; the chair is knocked over: the kitchen is empty. His daughter has fallen from the roof of their house and he is electric with life.

[PLATE 24]

"The Cotton Market, New Orleans"

1873, 29⅛ x 36¼

Sketches of fifteen figures were woven together into a single space. Fifteen figures, seized by the characteristics of their time.

Back in the day when cotton was stuffed into the necks of aspirin bottles by hand, your grandfather owned the top cotton-plug house in New Orleans. Perhaps it's hard to picture such a different time. You'll be better able to picture such a time if you take a moment to slow your mind down. Really slow the thoughts, make them pass through cold jelly, through clay, through liquid lead. Because the pace was much slower back then.

Because the pace was much slower back then, people weren't able to do very much. Time was practically at a standstill.

Imagine — slowly — thousands of slaves dedicated to a single task: the building of a pyramid. Twenty men pushing and pulling a single block of sandstone. They push and pull that single block of sandstone for their entire lives.

That's how New Orleans was in your grandfather's day. This was fine, of course. Back then, it was fine.

This anecdote isn't about time, though, so — well I guess I'm over-dwelling on just how slow life was in New Orleans, in your grandfather's day.

Your great-grandfather, from an even slower generation, was always at work first, because eight A.M. to him was five A.M. to your grandfather — you follow? Great-grandfather liked to examine the cotton as it was brought in each morning. Unfortunately, since he was at work so very early, the day's cotton wasn't there, so Great-grandfather had to make due with the cotton fibers he found left from the day before. He would sit on a hard wooden chair (all chairs were hard back then) and closely examine the fibers of cotton he'd collected from the corners of the cotton house.

Slavery, you might not know, is terrible.

When one thinks about New Orleans, and when one thinks about slavery, one can't help but think about voodoo. You're thinking about voodoo right now.

When your grandfather would arrive at eight, he came carrying the newspaper, finger to the page he'd left off on when he'd had to leave the breakfast table. Being of French descent, his pants were covered with flakes of croissant. He would sit just behind your great-grandfather and open the paper and pick up from where he left off. Soon, his employees would arrive, as would the daily bushel of cotton. His employees would say, "What's the news today?" and your grandfather would read aloud whatever had struck his fancy that morning.

Only one bushel of cotton a day was needed, because even though there were many bottles to plug, the pace in that day was so slow the day was over before they could get to a second bushel. By the end of the day, Great-grandfather was gone, because when it was only three P.M. for your grandfather, it was six P.M. for your great-grandfather.

The news in that day was often several days old.

For example: a man woke on Tuesday to discover an arm in his bed that was not his own. This was reported on Thursday. The story, fortunately, remained interesting, even though old. I'll tell it again: a man woke on Tuesday to discover an arm in his bed that was not his own. Indeed, the arm was as brown as tea leaves, and the arms of the man who woke beside the brown arm were the color of catfish bellies. So, imagine his surprise.

I am trying to make the past interesting to you. I am trying to make my own life seem real to you. My father was unable to make his life seem real to me. When, finally, the important question about my father arose: is my life like my father's, I found no answer. One day—how can you imagine this?—you'll ask the same of my life. I want you to be able to picture my life. To lay that picture upon yours, two texts on tissue paper. When you come to ask the question, you will see me as very old, a skull above my shoulder as clear a death-portent as any death-portent could be, and you'll wonder, how could that man have been a man? However could he have gone to work and married and had a son? You'll wonder, have I been different enough to avoid his fate?

I am like the zombies who toiled as slaves in New Orleans. I am slow and a slave to the time I was born in. I am so slow I can hardly be seen by you, except in the haze of your periphery.

[PLATE 25]

"At the Race Course"

1869–72, 18⅛ x 24

Movement is violent. So it is best for the slender horses and their jockeys to remain frozen. Degas watched the sun rise and set above the dusty racetrack, saw the crowd still in the slow moments after the race.

Here, the flora was so dense we were forced to walk sideways. Damp, dark leaves brushed our faces, stuck to our clothes, fell into our pockets. Sunlight hardly penetrated at all—occasional circles, yellow and white. "Are you sure we're on the trail?" my friend asked. We'd hiked for an hour already, our destination a forest-fire lookout tower—the view, I was told, was "the best." I wasn't sure, couldn't be, and said so, "but I think we're still on the trail, it's just overgrown and . . . . " My friend spoke over me: "Look at this." All I could see was the back of his jacket and the crown of his head which, as we stepped into the sunlight, became more blond, more blond; he stepped aside and I saw what lay ahead: a clearing, a wide, dirt path so dry it was white.

"Well this is something," I said.

My friend lit a cigarette. He inhaled, exhaled. He pointed with his cigarette and said, "What's that?"

Several tall figures stood hazy in the sun.

"Hello?" I said.

My friend strode toward the figures and disappeared into the sun. I put my hand to my forehead and could see him again and I wondered, "Where are we now?"

"These are carousel horses," he said.

I could see that he spoke but I couldn't hear my friend because he didn't call out, said to himself, "These are carousel horses." I caught up and saw what the figures were.

"These horses are wooden," I said.

"They're carousel horses," he said.

Astride each horse was a papier-mâché jockey. They'd once been brightly colored. The dirt path wasn't a path but a track. We've left the forest, I thought, though, in fact, we were in a clearing — the forest was all around us. Alongside the road was a length of split-rail fence. On the other side of the fence, flat on the ground, was a shiny piece of cut plywood. I crossed the road, hopped the fence and saw that the plywood was painted. I propped up the plywood.

"Hey," I called.

The plywood was cut and painted to look like a stand of empty bleachers. My friend laughed. On the grass were other cut-outs: men and women dressed in fashions from another century.

My friend stared at one of the jockeys, he smoked and he stared. He put the burning coal of his cigarette against the arm of one of the papier-mâché jockeys. Its arm lit instantly. To quell the fire, my friend knocked the arm off the jockey. "Damn," he said. Louder, he said, "They go up like mummies."

"Come on," I said. "We should go."

"What?" My friend said. He ran a finger along the cheek of a jockey.

"I said we should go." I added, to soften my insistence, "If we want to get to the tower and back before dark."

He looked at me a moment, looked at his watch. He looked at me.

We walked across the race track back into the forest.

The lookout tower stood at the top of a steep, narrow trail. I said, "The access road must be on the other side. We must've gone around backward." The trail was overgrown, and thick tree branches lay across it at regular intervals. "This trail is closed. This is what they do when they close a trail," I said.

"We can see the tower."

"I'm just saying."

"We can get to the tower."

We hiked up the hill until the tower stood large in front of us. Forest fire season was over, so the platform was locked up, a little trapdoor, padlocked, but the stairs and ladders among the tower's legs were unimpeded. We climbed up till we were just under the platform, and the view was very good, and I said so. I hooked my arm on a ladder rung and leaned out. A turkey vulture glided past at eye-level. We were a hundred feet from the ground.

My friend reached over the lip of the platform and felt around. Satisfied, he lit a cigarette—the wind where we were was steady but he lit a cigarette, held it firmly between his lips, gripped the edge of the platform with his fingers and swung from the ladder. My hands broke into a hot sweat. My friend pulled himself onto the platform.

He walked around the platform, stood on the spot above my head, put his lips to a space between boards and said, "You should come up here."

I said, "Have you thought about getting down?"

"There's a rope. Hold on a minute."

"Here." A rope crept into my line of sight. "Now you can swing out and climb up." My palms were so slick with sweat, I wasn't sure I'd be able to keep my grip, so I tied the rope around my waist and said, "Is it tied good? What do you have it tied to?" My friend shouted, "It's good, it's tied to the shed, just go!"

I swung out. For a long sick moment, the rope let out; it caught, at last, and I landed my feet against a leg of the fire tower. The tower swayed in the wind. When I felt steady enough, I climbed the rope and pulled myself onto the platform. "Took you long enough," my friend said. He said, "I wasn't sure I could hold on much longer." I saw then that the rope wasn't tied to anything. My friend had wound the rope around his leg and braced himself against a corner of the shed.

"You son of a bitch."

"I don't tie good knots."

"I threw all my weight out on that!"

"I know. You're heavy."

"You're insane."

"Come on. Take a look."

Rope still tied around my waist, I leaned over the railing. The mountain sloped green and cold — with my eye I followed the trail we'd hiked. The clearing, where we'd found the carousel horses, was not visible through the dark trees, but a trail of white smoke shone amid branches.

"What's that?" I said. My friend didn't hear me. I turned and looked at him: he looked peaceful, cigarette coiling smoke up past his face, a vacant stare. In an instant he'd be full tilt again. I was still angry. "Come over here," I said. I pointed at the smoke and now saw flames, a narrow trail of flames moving up the trail we'd hiked.

"What is that?" My friend asked. He leaned forward — I put my hand on the small of his back, nervous he'd carelessly throw himself over. "It's moving fast," he said. "In a straight line. That's not normal, is it?"

"I don't know," I said.

"I must not've," he said. "I must not've put out the fire."

A wind rushed over the fire tower and my friend's cigarette flared.

"There must've been an ember," he said.

The line of fire was closer. Black shapes were visible at the heart of the flames.

"We'll be safe where we are," I said, then thought better of this. "We've got to get out of here."

My friend bit down on his cigarette's filter. He said, "Finally."

"Finally what?" I shouted. I said, "Climb down on the rope with me." My friend leaned against the railing and crossed his arms. "You go down," he said. "I came here for the view. Look," he said.

I tied the rope to the railing, slid under the railing, lowered myself a few feet, swung until I caught the ladder, untied the rope from my waist and climbed down as quickly as I could, skipping rungs, picking up splinters, stumbling. The sound of the riders: horses whinnying, fire crackling, rushing air; men crying out to their animals, to the air, to the vultures.

[PLATE 26]

"Café Concert: The Song of the Dog"

1875–77, 21⅝ x 17¾

Here the singer mimics a dog: Degas confessed, somewhat backhandedly, "I have per-haps too often treated woman as an animal." I have heard his excuses all too often. The singer's illuminated face floats among the trees and leaves a pattern of glowing electric lights.

Young and married and with dog, a sleepy mutt, part Australian sheepdog, part some-thing else, maybe German shepherd, they go out after dinner for pastry at an outdoor café they like. The husband and wife walk with their dog between them, the sound of the café singer getting clearer and clearer.

" . . . friends," the husband says.

"Like?"

"Last night Carrie was in my dream. The night before, Jeff. Matthew peering in through our living room window. Kate. Marianne."

The married couple find a table along the outer edge of the patio. They like this par-ticular café because their dog is welcome. They come every Tuesday and other nights. On Tuesday evenings, the café hires a singer to provide live entertainment. Their dog sits with his head on the wife's left shoe. She tries not to move but sometimes jabs the dog a little; he snorts. He's disinclined toward agitation.

The husband says, "The dream-visits aren't always nice."

"How not nice?"

"They often seem annoyed, I guess. They seem...." The husband taps the tabletop. "I wake up." He runs his index finger in a circle. "I feel bad."

They order a thick slice of blueberry torte and two coffees. He drinks his with cream and sugar. The singer sings songs in French. The words mean nothing to the couple, so the singer's songs mix into the background noises at the outdoor café: rustling leaves, people talking, cell phones, plates against plates and silverware and coffee glasses, automobiles. The dog snorts. The dog closes his eyes. The singer's face is flat and flabby. Her chin is a little bump beneath her mouth.

The wife says, "Like, headaches?"

"No. Anxious."

"Why?" The wife's mouth is shaping to tease.

"I'm embarrassed to say."

A grin, she says, "You've told me this much." And, "Do you make out with Marianne in your dreams?"

"No."

"Then?" She doesn't understand where his story is going. Their torte comes. She digs right in; he sits back, watches her. He's trying to figure out how to explain. The dog's head is too warm on the wife's foot so she twists it free; the dog just lets his head lay on the patio slate. She feels a little bad, but her foot feels better. Surrounding the patio are round lamps. Quite a crowd has come to hear the singer. The singer is very enthusiastic. She waves her hands — she's wearing long, white gloves — she waves her hands as if she's dog paddling. Sometimes the wife thinks their dog must be incredibly bored by what she and her husband talk about. She tends to wonder this when she herself is bored. Or annoyed. She says, "I've been thinking that I'd like to move the painting we have in the bedroom out to the hall."

"Why?"

"I think we should move the painting in the bedroom out to the—"

"I heard what you said. I asked why, not what."

"Oh." She licks her fork for the third time. He hasn't touched it and she's had her share. She has another bite. "I'd like to put the mirror where the painting is."

"Oh?"

"Why not?"

"I've gotten used to the painting being there when I go to sleep."

"But the room's dark."

"I can make out shapes. I concentrate on it to get to sleep."

"Well, anyway, I'd like to have a mirror there."

The husband looks under the table at their dog. "We can take a look at that tomorrow."

"Okay."

The singer catches the couple's attention when she announces, in English, that the next song is for all the dogs in the audience. The singer says, "I know you're out there, sweeties."

The husband looks at the wife. The wife says, "She's sweet."

The singer begins to sing. The husband points to their dog. "He doesn't seem too interested." The wife pats the dog's head. The husband says, "So what do you think it means that I'm seeing so many friends in my dreams?"

The wife shrugs.

Their dog leaps up, bangs his head on the underside of the table, and points with his body at the singer. The couple follows their dog's gesture to the stage, and notice that though the singer is waving her arms and flapping her hands, and that though her mouth is wide open and her eyes squeezed shut, she isn't singing. At least there's no sound coming from her open mouth. Another dog on the patio barks; their dog barks.

The singer closes her mouth, opens her eyes and puts a hand to her throat. There is a smattering of applause. Their dog is jumping and panting.

The wife says, "Well that's bizarre." A waiter comes and removes the couple's dessert plate. The wife says to her husband, "I don't like that painting. And I'd like to be able to do my face in the bedroom where the dresser is."

The husband says, "You know what I keeping thinking? I keep thinking, you know, just before you die, aren't you supposed to see all your friends and relatives?"

[PLATE 27]

"The Tub"

1886, 23⅝ x 32⅝

The air is green fractured, the nude bather is lines of smoke and day's end: her left foot and hand, pink, and a slim line of hair tucked behind her ear; her buttocks, her back, her breasts, dun. Unfinished, but complete.

The overhead light flickers, blink, blink, a wavering yellow light in a gloomy house. I've found a chair I like, a rocking chair. When I'm sitting on this rocking chair, I don't have to do anything but rock. I don't read or eat or watch television. The television is a little black and white box, another incongruent detail in a rich woman's house. The floors were once green; flakes of paint trapped between the planks the only evidence of this now. Another incongruous detail. "I've been told," my girlfriend said to me, "that nothing about this house is casual. That is," she says, "to say the disrepair isn't in fact disrepair, but atmosphere. There," she points, "that yellow water stain is like a painting hung on the wall."

Yet much of the house grandly displays wealth. The couch my girlfriend is sitting on (she's reading) is massive green leather studded with copper. The Morisot sketch on the wall is a real Morisot sketch. The locked bookcase is full of rare books (my girlfriend has the key, she's reading a volume that crackles like bacon in her hands). The pay my girlfriend is getting to watch the house while its occupants are abroad is unreasonable.

I work at a video store. When I finish my shift I ride my bicycle to the house my girlfriend is currently employed by, carry my bike up the steps, ring the bell, and my girlfriend lets me in. I am content. The video store throws away its unpopular video-cassettes; I rescue them. My girlfriend and I watch them in the master bedroom where I've installed a VCR. The television in the master bedroom is color, but old. The green the television washes every picture with suits the old movies I bring home and fills me with a heavy nostalgia.

For what I can barely tell.

The movies are bad yet fascinating: characters act in ways that make no sense; stories end without ending, narrative threads are dropped, lost. These films vanish. Some of these films, my girlfriend says, are brilliant. Maybe I agree. With her, the more peculiar something is, the more it is to her taste. I'm not always sure my girlfriend is to my taste. I do not know her well. But she is quite beautiful, a dark-eyed girl who stares and stares and stares. She is distant, but we make love often. Her intellect is wholly unlike anyone's. I guess I'm afraid of her. When she opens the door there is nothing but darkness behind her. The video we watch ends and the room is dark.

My girlfriend twists the knob on an expensive lamp (real Tiffany) and there's a flare and a click-pop and both the overhead light and the lamp are dark.

My girlfriend finds a flashlight in a kitchen drawer and leads the way down the basement stairs.

We easily locate light bulbs, there are stacks and stacks of them, but a tin glint catches my eye and I say, "What's that?" My girlfriend shines her light over a metal tub. She turns the flashlight on her face and says, "That's a bathtub."

I don't think anything of it for a little while, just stare at her face, the lit bulbs of her cheeks, the lit plane of her brow, and then it dawns on me: How odd it would be to take a bath in a big tin bucket. And so my girlfriend must. We haul the tub up the stairs and put it in the living room near a low shelf that runs along the staircase. We boil water. Filling the tub is a slow process and I know my girlfriend appreciates this. "To run a bath is without effort. To make a bath takes time."

She drapes her clothes over the leather couch. She is naked in this strange living room and I am fully clothed. I watch. She says, "Are you just going to stand there?" She isn't inviting me to join her, she's asking to be left alone. The light in the living room is the color of the veins in my arms, a light that originates from nowhere or from the house or from my girlfriend. She says, "Would you turn on the lamp and hand me my book?" The rare book she reads in a tin tub. The lamplight spoils the room. I wander into the kitchen for something to eat.

When the bathwater goes cold, my girlfriend calls to me, "Come here and bring me a towel." She wears the towel up to the bedroom. We make love with the damp towel beneath us. The bedroom is full of furniture I've barely looked at; the bed isn't mine, the artful crack across the ceiling travels beneath rooms I've never seen. There is so much space in this house that I have not occupied and will not. I haven't been to my own apartment in days.

At the foot of the bed is the television. All around are white, plastic video cases; one, open: its shadow is the shadow of an open book. My girlfriend sleeps without covers even though it's cold. She sleeps with her hands folded on her belly.

I leave the bedroom very early, before she wakes. She's on her side, her back to me, a curved line of bone to the dark break of her buttocks and back again to the hollow where neck meets skull. I stop on the staircase that overlooks the living room because I am aware — aware like an animal — that the living room is not unoccupied. Below, a woman bathes herself in the tin tub. The air is green fractured; that single lamp with a green lampshade left on overnight. The woman's wet hair hangs over her shoulders.

She is washing her neck with a sponge. I look up the stairs toward the bedroom where my girlfriend is asleep and look back down on the woman in the tub, a woman with red hair, a woman as solid as the pale jade light that roams down her back as she stands.

[PLATE 28]

"The Bellelli Family"

1860–62, 78 ¾ x 99 ⅝

Against their ancestors play four brilliant figures. Against their forebears, the curve of their figures. Read the objects that surround the Bellelli family. Read the air that seethes a simple scene.

After the first explosion, the Bellelli family stood still and listened for further report: that is, proof that there was a first explosion. Mr. Bellelli sat gravely in his leather armchair. He held a pen over Sunday's unfinished sermon. Mrs. Bellelli's right hand rested lightly on the shoulder of her youngest daughter; her left hand was settled lightly on her husband's heavy desk. Her eldest daughter, the one-legged daughter, seated on a wooden chair, was stern, hands on her hips. She looked past her father, out the window. She saw that the trees in the backyard were half-uprooted, they leaned like loose teeth. She deluded herself into believing the trees in the backyard had always grown sideways. The youngest daughter, hands crossed over her stomach, stared at the ghost. The ghost had been stirred up from between the floorboards by the blast.

An aftershock, perhaps, the Bellelli family house tilted. Mr. Bellelli's chair canted back. The chair's weight kept him upright and serious. One false move and balance would be lost. To smile, for example. The youngest daughter broke from her mother's grip and ran after the ghost that chased itself out of the den. She cried out, "I see you!" The ghost was a-shimmer with embarrassment; it had never been seen before. Without the support of her youngest daughter, Mrs. Bellelli fell down. All around her a black cascade of her thick dress. The dress was so black it looked as if Mrs. Bellelli was standing in a hole. The one-legged daughter laughed at her mother. At the angle Mr. Bellelli sat, he could not reach to strike his daughter. He could not write his sermon, either.

The second explosion destroyed most of the Bellelli home. The den stood, an elegant room in the middle of a burnt-out estate, as absurd as a teacup in a cockfight. Mrs. Bellelli had once asked Mr. Bellelli if he thought the bombs would reach the West. Mr. Bellelli said, "No. Never. There's no need to bomb the West." Many in the West believed they were safe from attack. They didn't recognize themselves as a rotten core, making suicidal choices every chance they got. Mr. Bellelli's sermon began: "With the end will come extraordinary beauty. As the world is incinerated, time will slow to a crawl and we'll be able to read the objects around us like little poems. Bands of light will transform ordinary objects into brilliant lampposts on the way to paradise." When his congregation thought of ordinary objects, they didn't think of blenders or television sets. They thought of chairs and silver knives.

The one-legged daughter stood and said, "Where did my sister run off to?" The ground shook and the one-legged daughter fell. The mother laughed. The one-legged daughter screamed, "Why did you keep my leg in your womb?" The one-legged daughter's favorite game was "Christina's World." She would crawl through a nearby field to her house like Christina Olson did. When she played, she dressed as Andrew Wyeth would have painted her: a long skirt, a white blouse. From the field she'd cry out, "Mother, Mother."

The second explosion lifted the youngest daughter and tossed her where the field once was. She writhed on the burnt ground and ate ashes. She asked, "Ghost, are you taking all this down?" She used to run through the field and when she saw her sister crawling she would run away, afraid her one-legged sister would steal one of her legs. When she was told to pray before bed she would thank God quickly and then, every night, ask God to kill her mother with her sister's missing leg, and to strike down her father during Sunday service. God, she was told, worked in mysterious ways. When she didn't take out the trash, she would explain to her father, "I work in mysterious ways."

Then the youngest daughter died. The ghost was in the den.

From the floor, Mrs. Bellelli shouted, "Who can possibly be happy in the final moments of annihilation?" The one-legged daughter screamed, "Shut up! There are no bombs!" She tried, in vain, to delude herself into believing she was in the field playing "Christina's World." Her mother's dress foiled her delusion. Her mother's dress was a tar pit. The den was sinking. Mr. Bellelli stood. His chair fell over with a dull thud that seemed like no sound at all. He stood by the window and listened to his own breathing, his own heart beating. He hoped these sounds would prove to be lampposts. He counted seconds.

What the ghost didn't expect was that after the Bellelli family was finally gone, it remained.

[PLATE 29]

"Dancers at the Bar"

1876–77, 18⁷/₈ x 24³/₄

Dancers adjusting their slippers, stretching their muscles, practicing their positions at the bar. With a brush to green paper, Degas drew two girls, one more lightly, an echo of the other.

His last high school girlfriend had only one sister, one year younger, and he loved her too. His girlfriend's father made him mixed drinks — "Scotch & soda, son?" — her mother asked him his opinions about the president and popular music — she listened to his answers while she smoked Lucky Strikes. This girlfriend was sophisticated. She claimed to have fallen in love with him while watching him eat a plate of French fries in the school cafeteria — "With a fork, while everyone else was greasing it up with their fingers. You twirled half a fry in ketchup as if it were a knot of spaghetti." Unusual thinking, he knew, was a sign of sophistication. She wore a man's hat with a feather in the band. She wore mascara like Cleopatra — "Like Elizabeth Taylor," she said. She believed in Jesus, but a creative, real Jesus — "He was practically black" — and went to church on Sundays even though her parents and sister did not. He would see her hat among those at the front of the church; he and his mother sat far back, so they could beat "Catholic traffic." He longed to sit with her, but couldn't bring himself to broach the topic with his mother.

Several Sundays into their relationship, she introduced herself to his mother. His mother gushed and invited his girlfriend to sit with them and she did. Religion had never felt so great. Later, his mother said, "Your girlfriend is like a silent film actress." He and his girlfriend spent hours talking, making imaginary plans for the future, complaining about conformity, proposing collaborative artistic ventures.

His girlfriend took dance classes, and — as she did everything — she took dance very seriously. Her sister danced, too.

His girlfriend's father gave him his first suit — "It'll be a little large on you, son, but I used to wear this, in my trimmer days." The suit was too large, but not absurdly so. He wore the suit to his girlfriend and her sister's dance recitals — everyone else in the audience wore jeans and button-down shirts. He loved watching his girlfriend and her sister dance. They moved within a circle of their own making; the audience, the other dancers, street noise, etc. couldn't penetrate their circles. Sometimes their dance instructor complained that they appeared out of synch with the girls. His girlfriend's sister said, "Our instructor doesn't like how we dance because we make the other girls look bad." This was true: the other girls in the class too often looked at each other and were perpetually a step behind the music. His girlfriend and her sister's circles held the music, kept count. They understood why they moved when they did, while the other girls did what they were told because they were told.

On his birthday, his girlfriend danced for him.

He wore his suit and they went to the diner they liked and she paid (her mother had slipped her a twenty). After dinner and coffee they drove back to her house and she danced for him, in her bedroom. Her bedroom was papered, on three walls, with green paper, ribbed like corduroy. The fourth wall was a mirror. A dance bar was attached; both his girlfriend and her sister had similar set-ups so they could practice. Their bedroom floors were hardwood. When his girlfriend stood in front of the mirror she was in a green field, in a jungle, within a great, monochrome painting. She danced there, a creature wholly in its element, moving for the pleasure of doing so. He spent the night in her bed, as he did when he could. They kissed until they fell asleep, hot and exhausted.

During summer vacation he was invited to join his girlfriend's family at the summer house they'd rented. He didn't need permission to go; his mother would be glad to have him gone. He didn't have clothes suited to a stay in a seaside town, and he worried about this, because he didn't have money to rectify the problem. His girlfriend said, "What do you think, I want you in white trousers?"

He marveled that his girlfriend and her sister never fought. They consulted each other regarding even personal matters. Many of his friends had siblings they hated, or siblings they loved but didn't like. His girlfriend and her sister shared clothes, stolen Lucky Strikes, friends, and most of all, dance. In the narrow kitchen of his girlfriend's parents' summer house, the two girls danced to the radio, a brand new song with a fuzzy beat and robot-voiced lyrics. The way they moved in a narrow space: narrow waists, slim, slow arms, long, dark hair, feet planted.

Though, with the help of his girlfriend, his grades had vastly improved as had his SAT scores, he was not eligible for scholarships. He would go to a state school. His girlfriend had been offered two scholarships at private colleges. He knew she would accept one and be gone. He suggested to her that she consider herself single when she went, that long-distance relationships were too hard. He wished she would disagree, but she was sophisticated enough not to; so, she would go as if single, with the glimmer of hope that seeing each other over winter break might change their minds: a hope they both held. When it was time for her to leave, he and she packed up her room. Put into plastic milk crates what she would take to her dorm room — "You'll have to come visit" — "Yes. I will." Before her parents called them down for dinner, she stretched on the dance bar. In the mirror, her other self stretched on the dance bar. She performed for him the dance she'd danced on his birthday.

At dinner her family was jovial enough, though he caught their sad glances.

He spent the night in his girlfriend's bed; her parents knew. Their daughter did as she pleased, and somehow, what she did was usually wise; she was wiser than her young parents had been at her age.

He visited his now ex-girlfriend's parents several times after she left for college. He asked her parents for advice, for help when it looked as if he wouldn't pass mathematics. Her sister kept him abreast of the doings at high school. He went to her recitals.

One evening he showed up for dinner. His ex-girlfriend's parents weren't in—out grocery shopping, perhaps—he'd been invited. In his pocket was a small amount of cocaine he'd been waffling about all afternoon. A freebie, from someone on campus. He hadn't tried it, but he hadn't flushed it either. About to sit down on the couch and watch television, he heard a sound like stocking feet upstairs. At the foot of the stairs to the second floor, he heard music. His ex-girlfriend's sister must be practicing in her room. He went up. The sister's room was unoccupied—yellow wallpaper, wood floor, mirrored wall. The music came from his ex-girlfriend's room. He felt a rush of hope and happiness; he opened the door and she was there, stretching on the bar, green all around her, as if she danced inside an emerald. The only light in the room came from the windows, gray light, winter light. He watched her dance. He heard the sound of her footfalls. Her hair swung free, fanned out, made a rope, made a black-bristled paintbrush. When she came out of her circle, she saw him in the mirror and smiled. "My parents should be back soon." The dancer was his ex-girlfriend's sister—no surprise—but he was glad and grateful for the illusion.

[PLATE 30]

"Breakfast after the Bath"

1883, 47 7/8 x 18 1/4

The nude, a nude woman — her nervous outline, hues laid one over another. That is to say, the nude woman Degas painted was modeled by broken color.

A thick line of porcelain between the bather's legs: the bather straddles the lip of the freestanding tub. The air in the cabin is cool and steam rises from the bather and the bath. She leans forward and lifts a towel from a folded stack on the floor. She kicks open another towel, spreads it open with her foot. Jules, the bather's baby son, sleeps.

The bather gathers her hair in her left hand. She holds her hair up off her neck and her shoulders. The bather's mother says, "I brought you tea." The bather's mother stands a little behind the bather. The cabin is small; a hunter's retreat. There is no bathroom, no kitchen, no bedroom. The floor is covered with carpets: strewn. Outside, the snow falls and is deep on the ground.

"Not now."

Steam plays with the light, carries light shimmering green and white. The windows fog and condensation weeps lines from latch to sill.

"Okay," the bather's mother says. And: "Breakfast is ready. Jules is asleep." She sips the tea she made for the bather.

The bather wraps her hair in a towel. She turns, nude as the baby boy across the room, the baby sleeping on the only bed in the cabin. The bather bends at the waist, picks up the towel she'd spread on the floor and wraps it around her body.

The bather's mother has prepared a pot of creamed wheat. The sun clears the room of steam. Lines of light fall across the walls of the cabin, light speckled with the gray shadows of window water drops.

Holding a spoonful of creamed wheat close to her mouth the bather whispers, "Jules." Her son's name blows heat from her food. The bather looks across the room at her son. Her mother looks up; her mother looks down at her food. Too hot to eat quickly, their breakfast will be cold before they're done. Jules gurgles. The cabin, the bather's mother thinks, is a safe-house. The bather's mother thinks, "How could my daughter marry a man who isn't a man?"

"The snow," the bather's mother thinks, "will throw him off our trail. He's a hot-weather beast, a spring animal."

The bather takes the spoonful of food into her mouth. The taste is like her baby's breath. From her mouth she draws a bare spoon. The bather taps the spoon against her teeth. She thinks, "My husband will find us." She says, "Mother, isn't there any sugar in the cabin?"

The cabin is nearly bare, so they will have to move on, or at least they will have to go out for supplies. One or the other. The bather doesn't want to leave yet. For the moment, the bather feels secure. The bather and her mother sit at the little wooden table for an hour, bowls empty.

"At least," thinks the bather, "I make Jules' food."

The bather takes the towels from her head and body and drapes them over the lip of the bath. She puts on a blue, flannel, shapeless dress. She joins Jules on the bed. There's very little for her to do in the cabin, little left to be said. Talk invariably leads to panic. What prospects have they? What chance of escape? The bather dozes with her baby. The bather's mother sits in a chair by the window. The falling snow lures the bather's mother into a daze.

The bather sees in her mind a giant white blade of grass, a line like the edge of the bathtub. She stands before the white blade of grass. Jules coos, she cups his head; both actions are without intention.

The giant blade of grass is a wall between sleep and awake "a blade of grass as big as I am." The bather sees what's on the other side of that wall: a great writhing passage of dull green vines.

The bather's mother sees the snow cease to fall, to melt; she sees green shoots break from the muddy yard around the cabin, she sees a great forest close over them, the eyelid of a sleeping beast.

[PLATE 31]

"A Ballet Seen from an Opera Box"

1885, 25 ¹/₈ x 19 ¹/₄

As once he sketched me, partially obscured by a bend in the corridor at the Louvre, he allowed the world to interfere with his subjects. Never before were featured figures so fragmented. Many of Degas' friends honored this skew: Toulouse-Lautrec, especially. Absolute realism is always deeply strange.

Brother and Sister and their current respective significant others (who shall remain nameless and will not be mentioned again) sat in the front row of the ballet, those good tickets a gift to Brother, a business perk. Both Brother and Sister disliked the front row, always preferring the balcony where they'd sat for shows since childhood. The front row embarrassed Sister and put a crick in Brother's neck; however, he did find the angle at which he was forced to gaze at the ballerinas . . . enlightening.

The day before the ballet Brother and Sister went to a bookstore together laughing as they often were: Brother caused Sister to laugh at inappropriate times, always the best laugh. They spent some time browsing. Books as so many knickknacks, possessing so little of the energy books ought, dressed with eye-catching designs. (Sister kept count: Brother pointed out nineteen books as "interesting" with nude or nearly nude women on the cover, women severed by title and author, by logo and line.) Sister went up to a clerk, a middle-aged woman who seemed pleasant enough. Sister said, "I'm looking for a book." The clerk waited for Sister to say more and waited. Sister said, "It's . . . a book." Over the clerk's face fell a shadow of book-clerk rage and then a different shadow crept from chin to scalp. The clerk said, "Yes," and walked off. Sister elbowed Brother, thinking she'd played her joke and that the joke had played out, but the clerk came back with a book and put it in Sister's hand. "We had it in overstock," the clerk said.

Crucial to the clerk's joke — Sister and Brother were sure they'd been had and appreciated having been had (so often they were left to their own devices) — crucial to the clerk's joke was the book. The book could've been a dubious paperback which would have been the clerk's way of saying to Sister, "I don't think you're all that smart, Miss." It wasn't such a book. The Bible would have been a suitable response: a book called The Good Book and a way for the clerk to say, "Get some Christ in your life and maybe you won't be such a jerk," but the book wasn't The Bible. The book could've been self-help, "You need it," or a how to lose weight guide or a guide to manners, "Which you are apparently without." Instead:

The book was a hardcover collection of newspaper articles from a local paper neither Brother nor Sister knew; a small-time paper honored by a small press. The book Sister had been given seemed like no joke so Sister bought the book. The dust-jacket was a reproduction of a front page from many years ago: "Dorset Building to Be Demolished" the headline.

A ballerina approached the edge of the stage and leaned forward, smiling, seemingly at Brother. Her face was cast in yellow light, a ghastly light. Behind her a dozen blue ballerinas. Brother looked away, into the orchestra pit. Behind a cellist, was an open, little door, revealing a set of stairs beneath the stage. "There lives the machinery of this dance," Brother thought. He sketched with his fountain pen onto his program the door and the stairs. He crosshatched shadow: light at the door, black where the stairs vanished. As he drew, he thought of an article he and Sister read in the newspaper book they'd bought. They'd read the book together on a park bench, the book open across their laps.

The article he remembered had caused them both to look up. The headline: "Man Shot, Transformed into Whale." The story: Three men were sitting at a round table. The table was on a beach, close to the water. The table was sinking into the sand. One man reminded the other men that he knew all about their unsavory activities. He knew of their activities because he had made the arrangements for said activities. He told the other men that he could easily blackmail them, but that he wasn't going to. The two men who had engaged in unsavory activities looked at each other. One of the two shot the man who had mentioned blackmail. The shot man rose from his chair and transformed into a humpback whale. For a moment the whale stood upright on its flukes, then toppled, driving the table into the sand and crushing the surprised men. From its mouth frothed forward red plankton.

Brother passed his sketch to Sister, expecting she too would think of the man transformed into a whale. Then a radical shift in point-of-view occurred: not from third to second or first, but in space. Sister projected herself—Brother's program and graffiti in hand—into one of the balconies above and behind Brother and Sister's seat. From the first row, Sister could not see the balcony, but she knew it so well it was easy for her to be in that balcony and see what she would see from that balcony. The balcony was not high in the opera house, but a first-tier balcony, so Sister was close to the audience on the ground. A woman's fan opened boldly in Sister's low-periphery. Around the woman with the fan the audience burbled darkly. A ballerina in yellow leaned forward in Brother's direction and Brother's eyes drifted away from her yellow face to the orchestra pit. A dozen blue ballerinas crossed the stage behind the yellow ballerina.

Now firmly in her front row seat, Sister looked at Brother's drawing of the little doorway. She could not, from where she sat, see the doorway. She stared at the dense thicket of crosshatched black lines where the stairs vanished and, as a banner of text across the inside of her brow, she saw a headline from the newspaper book she and

Brother had read together in a park the day before. The headline she saw was the headline on the last page of the book: "Newspaper Publisher Found Guilty." Of what, the accompanying article did not disclose.

[PLATE 32]

"The Café Singer"

1878, 20¼ x 16

Before there were movies there were stage shows and Degas attended those. For now, forget the ballet. Lipstick redder than any woman's hair. Fur, and blonde, and pink. This vulgar singer's black glove haunted Toulouse-Lautrec, who so often drew it floating among the rafters of the woods.

His last unemployment check (for real, this time) coincided with the first letter from the IRS. The IRS queried about his failure to file—six years in a row. The time to pack his car and leave his apartment in the low city was come. He didn't pack much—he didn't *have* much—but still too much. A hundred miles north, when he finally stopped at a gas station, he left a stack of books and a clock in a neat pile in the men's room. (The clock was a gift from a girlfriend, "So you'll be on time for work." The clock had failed to change him.)

He'd meant to escape earlier. It was late afternoon.

His trip north thrummed along. He didn't eat much. He didn't stop to stretch. He listened to the same cassette, turning it over and over. For long stretches, he drove in silence.

His escape was futile. He couldn't escape desperation.

Out loud, he asked himself, "Is death certain?" After all, he hadn't paid taxes in some time. "Is death certain?" Death couldn't be proved certain until he died; "I might be the first to live forever." At times he'd felt hopeful that eternal life was just around the corner. He glanced at the road map on the passenger seat to determine the most obscure route north. Far enough and he couldn't drive any further. He believed death was certain. "Some people," he thought, "believe their spirit is reborn to this world again and again; therefore death is only transitional." He thought that philosophy overly optimistic. A paradise with God was even more optimistic and so less plausible. The cure for death struck him as an absurd phrase. He said it out loud, "The cure for death." He said, "The cure for death" until he couldn't stand the dumbness of that phrase.

Then he listened to the cassette in the stereo once more.

The fuel light came on so he stopped at a gas station. He left a box of clothes in the men's room.

He couldn't quite walk over the gulf of fear that was open beneath him, or drive away from that which pressed against his back. In the rear-view mirror he saw he'd been nowhere.

Somewhere, in a forest in Maine, he set up his tent. He planned to leave when he woke in the morning. He didn't. He spent the day sleeping and worried that his tent would be found and so the illusion of being nowhere, untethered, would be destroyed. The fabric of his tent was green, so the light inside his tent was green. He floated there, the fear of the outside encroaching a dim line around the edge of his suspension, his contented lack of place.

"Where is there singing?" he asked himself in a whisper.

"Outside," he replied. Outside the tent was miles of forest. Fifty miles to the east was the Atlantic. The ocean left traces deep in the forest: oyster shells, dried seaweed in the trees, pink crab claws. The singing meant other people were nearby and this was disappointing, he didn't want to be found, but the voice was lovely. So lovely, in fact, the words sung were unintelligible, the words lost in the hum and whir of a throat.

He unzipped his tent and followed the voice. Night had fallen; without the voice, the forest would be totally dark. His walk took him in and out of dense wood. He heard nothing but the voice, not the muttering of animals or the muttering of his thoughts. He didn't know how long he walked or how far he was from his tent. The bones in his legs ached. He saw, ahead, the source of the voice that had lured him from his tent.

In a clearing stood a stage, red curtains drawn, a woman behind a microphone. She sang. Her hair was tied back with a black ribbon. In the spotlight projected from nowhere her black gloves glowed.

He stood in the clearing as far from the stage as he could but still he grew closer until he stood at the singer's feet. She looked down and smiled through her song. She raised her hand and opened her mouth wide for a long note and from her mouth emerged a bird. The bird, red, wet from the woman's throat, pushed itself from the woman's mouth and flew up, hovered above the woman's head and flew away. The song was gone. The woman stood frozen, a hollow thing made of wood and cloth.

[PLATE 33]

"The Mante Family"

1889, 25 ⅛ x 19 ¼

The Mante Family: the father played in the orchestra and three of his daughters were ballet dancers. Here, Suzanne is dressed for practice; Blanche stares the stare. What of la mère? *She fastens. Ribbons and bows.*

We never thought we would live to the new century, even though we were young at the end of the old and so odds were in our favor.

✦ ✦ ✦

Suzanne is seven and ready to audition. She'll audition with the "Danseuse" dance which she'll practice with red ribbons and a diaphanous green — oh, but green so pale — tutu. Suzanne's sister Blanche on the couch will keep count. Father will muscle the few notes of import: listen to the big boom, the second crash, the sixth silent note and the pretty music that follows the messy music. Suzanne will practice with Father's music and to Mother's grunting and clapping. Father and Mother clear the floor of the apartment living room — a polished parquet floor — and Suzanne learns a dance akin to the "Danseuse" dance. An off-balance dance. Blanche, white, dressed in blood red and black ribbons: mother makes the ribbons from very tiny ribbons.

✦ ✦ ✦

We find remembering the first eight months of the new century difficult. Those months absorbed by a handful of quiet days abuzz with newscasts and nervous conversation.

✦ ✦ ✦

Suzanne and Blanche are two of three sisters. The third sister is never around anymore. She stayed in Cleveland or Omaha where the Mante family is from. She has her own apartment. At least, that's what the Mante family believes, based on recent reports. Blanche dreamed that her older sister fell apart, quite literally, like a Lincoln Log house yanked at its foundation, a little collapsing building. Her sister's face buried in a pile of limbs.

✦ ✦ ✦

The audition is an exceptional success. The famous choreographer is absolutely in love with Suzanne and the Mante family gladly gives Suzanne over to art. They will become a smaller family, an accomplishment.

✦ ✦ ✦

Before the audition, Suzanne, Blanche, and Mother stood by the wall, readying Suzanne. Blanche, in blood red and black ribbons, stared blankly ahead, clearing the room of all obstacles. Suzanne practiced her positions: first position, "I dance for God"; second position, "Prepare"; third position, "Work from pictures in your mind"; fourth position, "Bumping into walls"; and fifth position, "Sunk into the bones of dancing, they were going to Heaven."

Before Suzanne stepped from the wall to audition, Mother tested Suzanne's ribbons and whispered into her ear; Father knew what Mother whispered because it was what Mother whispered when she wished to grant success:

* * *

Let me tell you what the world is like. The world is buzzing with glacial joy, the Spring and the machines we humans build. The sky is bright and full of birds and airplanes. Politics are dumb and art is a belovéd wash of watercolor paint all over our faces and beneath our feet.

book three

HENRI DE TOULOUSE-LAUTREC

[PLATE 34]

"Young Routy"

1882, 23⁵/₈ x 19¹/₄

All around the brim of this young man's hat are the gold and soot-blackened gold of his thoughts. His thoughts are: the idea of self, the face of a young woman and the small of her back, and the certainty that the barbs of youth prick and poison.

Routy and I are too old for exploring; it's our first year of college; but these motions. We leap from stone to stone and over a stream. I swing myself up onto a tree that's fallen over. The tree's thick trunk is cracked. From the stump, green branches, ring by ring. Coils of vine. The tree's leaves are still green. Routy and I are in his parents' backyard. We're on vacation. Long weekend. I'd no other place to go, my friends went away. His parents suggested we come, eat from their fridge, relax.

Routy is wearing a striped shirt, a thin black tie, and a wide-brimmed hat that was his grandfather's. He's been wearing that hat around campus. We're all making ourselves up, now that we're out of high school, now that we're meeting new people in a new town. I took a corduroy sport jacket from my father's closet.

This yard isn't like a yard. This yard is a wild garden. Thick, furry plants glow in the sun and we pick blackberries from tangles of brambles. There's a ramshackle shed, wood warped and weatherworn gray. Along the shed's foundation are tomato plants.

Their vines have grown free and their fruit has tumbled to the ground. Against the shed is a bench.

Routy sits on the bench. I've too much energy to do so. Sunlight, broken by the wrecked roof edge of the shed, falls over Routy's hat. The patterns of light writhe on the black felt. Coil and uncoil. Routy tells me that he and his mother would pick blackberries together when he was a boy, that there were never enough for a pie.

Routy says, "There's a girl in my dorm."

I step back. His face is revealed from beneath his wide-brimmed hat. Shadow rings his eyes.

He says, "She paints."

Though there must be a hundred girls at our college who paint, I'm sure I know the girl who paints he's talking about.

He says, "She's really talented."

I say, "I love girls who paint."

He says, "She's beautiful."

I say, "I love the jeans they wear. Paint-splattered borrowed boys' jeans. You can always see their underwear." I can picture her. I say, "What's her name?" I'm not surprised when he tells me her name. I spent a night crashed out on the floor of her dorm room.

He says, "I think I might ask her out."

"Sure," I say.

"For coffee."

"Yeah."

I can't decide if I should tell Routy that she asked me why I would hang out with him and why does he wear that stupid hat? She wore jeans and red underwear and a short striped shirt. She told me the shirt was a kid-size rugby she got at the second-hand store on dollar-a-pound day. I didn't say Routy's hat was stupid, but I didn't say it wasn't. A shrug was my best explanation for why I was friends with him.

I reach to pick up something shiny in the tall grass by my feet — a sharp sting on my hand and I shout out. Routy jumps up and says what.

I see a little snake slither away. "That snake bit me." We gotta grab that snake, I think. "Get it," I shout and I'm on my feet and we're rushing around the shed trying to catch it.

Routy sees it move toward the tomatoes. The snake isn't moving that fast. I can't grab it because I won't: every time it's in reach I hesitate. The snake vanishes under the shed. I try to decide if I should go into the shed after it.

Routy says, "Forget it. It's just a garter snake." We go in to wash our hands for the lunch his mother is certainly making.

[PLATE 35]

"Portrait of the Artist's Mother Reading"

1887, 21¼ x 17¾

Wan morning light makes green gray. There is red, though, red as dark as real cherries.

The artist's mother reads a mystery novel. The artist is in another room typing on his mother's electric: a hum, a click, his progress slow. His mother doesn't hear him mumble over every word he snaps onto paper and she doesn't hear the typewriter or the creaking from the old wooden chair where her son is seated. She doesn't smell hot ink. The artist's mother is seated in her favorite reading chair, grass-green, worn soft to the touch but a firm support. "What is a chair?" the artist wonders.

The artist's mother lives in a building connected to another by a spider's thread.

The artist's mother is smiling over her mystery novel. On the cover of her book is a picture of a skeleton wearing a red smoking jacket, seated at a great oak desk, a large pistol on the blotter. Behind the artist's mother, above a little table, is a window. The view from that window—if the eye follows the spider's thread-line—is of another window. On the other side of that window is another mother, also seated in a favorite chair, also reading a paperback novel. In that other mother's apartment labors another artist, pounding on another typewriter. This artist's fingers move more easily, there is no mumbling over the novel that's steadily growing larger, a pile of typewritten sheets neat on a desk corner. This artist's mother isn't smiling.

The artist's mother's mystery novel is part of a series she's especially fond of. The heroine is the young great-granddaughter of a master detective. She channels his advice from "the other side" whenever she's on a really difficult case (she's always on a really difficult case) and sometimes his spirit helps her out of a tough scrape. The heroine, when just a little girl, was an award-winning horse-jumper until one summer she fell and broke her legs. Her legs never grew any longer after the accident, so she has the upper body of a woman supported by the legs of a twelve-year-old girl. (In every book, a man is put off by the heroine's deformity, only to come to his senses and fall madly in love with her.) The artist's mother doesn't like to read her son's novels. They start one way and go another.

Sunlight brings out the grain in the wood of the little table and the wax patterns worked into it. Light startles the spider's thread.

The other mother is dressed like the artist's mother. A blue shirt buttoned high around her throat. A billowy skirt. There's coffee on the table beside her. Reading what she's reading is exhausting. The steady thrum of the typewriter in the other room is maddening. "When will she stop writing?" the other mother wonders. She gets up and looks out the window. She sees the artist's mother reading. "Why does she mock me?" The stagnant air between the two buildings is stirred by a breeze: the spider's thread shivers and the other mother sees it for the first time. She opens her window and touches the thread—it sticks to her finger for a moment. She touches the thread again. She puts her weight on the thread. "Impossible," she thinks. The other mother gets up onto the widow sill—crouches on the window ledge. She puts her foot on the spider's thread and it holds her weight. "Where is the spider that made this?" she thinks.

The artist's mother puts her book down for a sip of tea. Her son belts out a string of curses. She hears pages thrown about, the electric typewriter crashes to the floor. She shakes her head and tut-tuts. She thinks, "Soon. Soon something is going to give."

[PLATE 36]

"The Laundress"

1889, 36⅝ x 29½

The object is the laundress, though one might say otherwise if asked: the object is brown and many shades of brown, even brown so bright it's red; the object is a white blouse worn and a white blouse lain on a table; or, the object is mademoiselle's der-riere. However, the object is what the laundress sees, and how she sees it. I see the precedent of Degas, who towers, quite literally, over Toulouse-Lautrec.

The girl's uniform had to be washed, *had* to be: no amount of talcum powder could change that, but the washing machines in the cellar were on the fritz again, so she had to walk to the laundromat. Her mother wouldn't give her a ride. The sun was up, the sky bald blue; a canary yellow tree among green. The sidewalk shimmered. She had to go to work in three hours but first she had to go to the laundromat.

She thought, "What a beautiful morning," and she thought, "I wish I didn't have to do my laundry," and she thought, "I wish I didn't have to go to work," and she thought, "I wish on my days off I would wake up early and take this same walk." She knew herself well enough to know that was never going to happen. On her days off she needed the whole morning to recover from the night before. "Why can't I change my life?" she thought, and so on and so forth.

The girl was paranoid that a pair of her panties would fall from her laundry bag, so she kept turning around. The sidewalk shimmered: no underpants.

She had just invested in *good* panties. No Hanes Her Way. No Costco multi-pack. These panties she'd invested in were brightly colored, words such as "cherry" and "organic" were embroidered on the crotch; these panties were thongs, low rise, bikini-style, and so on and so forth. She felt daring when she went to buy them and was disappointed and relieved when a female clerk rang up her purchase.

She had hopes, had the inkling, that someone other than her and (unfortunately) her mother might see her new panties.

The laundromat smelled of dryer sheets and popcorn. Colorful lint drifted through the air. Sorting clothes seemed to her wasted effort; all of her clothes went into a double-loader. She punched her clothes into the tightly packed washer.

She had brought homework. She'd brought the homework with the best of intentions, but at the laundromat there were so many distractions. Television. *Vogue* and *Elle*, which she could never afford to buy, and today:

A woman with short red hair. The woman leaned on a table, palms flat to Formica, finger tips at the aluminum edge of the table. The woman stared out the big laundromat window. She wore a white blouse, sleeves rolled once, twice above her wrists. She wore a skirt, nothing special, brown, knee length, loose. The woman's face was what caught the girl's fancy. Forehead and eyes obscured behind feathery bangs. A small, firm-but-round chin; her nose like her chin. The girl wasn't sure if she heard the woman humming or if it was only the machines. The sun warmed the woman's white face.

The woman's blouse was slightly see-through — the girl followed the line of the woman's bra, from back to breast. This intimate eye contact —

The girl's legs were bouncing up and down.

The woman's blouse clung a bit to her lower back.

The woman's blouse was so thin that the girl could see the woman's stomach, illuminated by that sun which lit the woman's face and caught lint as lint lazily drifted in the air. The woman's stomach was round and the girl imagined putting her hand on the woman's belly and when she realized what she was thinking she turned away and stared at her book. Stared vacantly, though. Stared not at all but went an embarrassed blank. The girl looked at the woman again. The girl wondered if her own breasts would grow any larger or if she would be flat for the rest of her life.

The woman bit her lower lip, tugged her lower lip into her mouth and the girl felt herself get flush all over. Her skin hot and antsy. The girl opened and closed her legs.

The girl's double-loader stopped rumbling. The girl stood — a little cautious, unsure about her footing, uncertain how the scissor of her walk would make her feel. Behind the double-loader, a wall of washers between the girl and the woman, the girl began to collect herself as she reached into the washer and collected her clothes. She looked around. A man was seated beneath the wall-mounted television. From where he sat, the girl thought, he can see us both.

The burden of work, of doing her laundry, was forgotten.

In a basket-cart, the girl brought her clothes to a dryer near the woman.

As the girl brought her wet clothes to the dryer, a pair of her new panties fell to the ground. Instead of quickly snatching them up, she ignored them, left them on the floor for the woman to see, perhaps to pick up and hand to the girl.

The woman didn't move, just continued to stare out into the sunlight. Across the street a tree had gone brown and red. A worn, pale blue sedan shone dully.

Once the rest of her wash was in the dryer, the girl picked up her panties. As she unbent upright, she noticed the man. He grinned. His eyes were on her panties. So surprised by this, the girl stood a moment, panties held out in front of her as if intentionally a display for the man.

She balled up her underpants and threw them into the dryer.

And she thought, "You filthy pervert," and, "I have to go to work," and, "I have to drag all this shit back home," and, "Why did he have to be here?" She sat in a white plastic chair and glared at her clothes through the circular window in the dryer.

A washer buzzed, indicating the end of a cycle. The woman broke off her reverie to retrieve her wash. The woman — hardly aware of the girl at all — brushed past the girl. A thigh to the girl's arm. The woman's skirt rough against the girl's bare arm and the girl thought, "My skin is burning my muscles are tense," and her skin was burning and her muscles were tense.

All her new panties tumbled in the dryer, bright lights of silk and cotton.

[PLATE 37]

"Cirque Fernando"

1888, 38³/₄ x 63¹/₂

A whip makes a line through a circus round; candy stripes suggest a frantically hap-py vacation with the kids. Onlookers see the cropped influence—via Degas—of those Japanese prints that famously traveled to Paris during the late 1800s.

My sister and I sat on the floor of our aunt and uncle's living room. Our parents were on a small, ornate couch with iron lion's paws for feet. Two of our cousins, a brother and sister, who we'd met for the first time at dinner, were on the floor with us. They were older than me and my sister, but younger than our parents and our aunt and un-cle, who were even older than our parents. The room was small. The carpet was green with a floral pattern. The room was full of books; there were bookcases against every wall, some with glass doors, and there were books in stacks on the floor. All kinds of books. Science fiction books caught my eye the most, but there were old books with gold letters on the spine and mystery novels and textbooks. The bookcases had match-ing sets. Encyclopedias, I guessed. But one series had Napoleon on the spine of every volume and I guessed those couldn't have been encyclopedias.

On one of the shelves was a ceramic horse, which my sister and I had laughed at before we sat down for dinner because it had a huge rear end and a big penis, too, with large testicles. All I had to do was look at my sister and then up at the horse and she would crack up.

Our cousins told us that they worked for a circus. Not a full circus, but a small circus that did shows inside of theaters. I thought it was very weird having relatives in the circus, and I could tell that my sister did too. My sister asked what kind of animals they had in their circus.

Our girl cousin said, "We don't have animals in our circus."

My sister was incredulous. This was really absurd, and I could tell she was starting to think there was no circus at all, because she glanced around at our aunt and uncle and mom and dad to see if they were laughing. They weren't. My sister asked, "What do you do in a circus without animals?"

Our boy cousin leapt to his feet and said, "Aha." He crouched down and leaned forward until he was on all fours. His pants stretched over his bony thighs and behind. Our parents and aunt and uncle looked surprised. He walked around the room like this, on all fours, effortlessly. Our girl cousin stood now. She was petite and very thin and wearing black stirrup pants with her shoes and socks off. She pretended she had a whip and went, "Snap!" Our boy cousin, responding to her command, did a backwards flip. My mother gasped. I was sure that he was going to hit the ceiling lamp with his feet, but he didn't. He landed on all fours, and padded around a little more. Our aunt looked startled. Our uncle looked a little dour, and clutched his drink. Our girl cousin went, "Snap, snap!" and our boy cousin froze. She jumped up, and landed on his butt, and stood there, perfectly balanced. She stood straight and went, "Hup!" and our boy cousin began to trot around the room. Each time he bounced up, I was sure her head was going to hit the ceiling. They moved around the room, and she said to my sister, turning her head so she could keep eye contact, "Normally I would be wearing a sequined leotard and my brother would be dressed all in brown."

Our girl cousin stretched out her arms and when they were about to pass the ceramic horse, I could see that she would for sure knock it off the shelf. And I hoped she would. I wanted her to smash the horse on the floor.

But she put her hands to her sides with a loud slap, and her brother stopped moving. She bounced off of him and he stood up and they both took a deep bow. Our father and our aunt began to clap, and then our mother. Our uncle kind of clapped, but was really just tapping his fingers against his glass. My sister and I didn't do anything, we were so amazed.

Eventually my sister said to our girl cousin, "So that's your circus?"

Our girl cousin leaned forward, bringing her face really near my sister's and said, "Yes, my little cousin, this is our circus."

[PLATE 38]

"A Corner in the Moulin de la Galette"
1892, 40 x 39

A glass of absinthe illuminates a corner . . . casts all in its green color. Even the great black coat is flecked green. How, then, does the table remain so sickeningly yellow? No matter: the table, sickeningly yellow.

The café is busy.

Seated alone, a young woman is hunched over a glass of blue-raspberry soda. Her jacket is emerald green. Her chin is very weak: she has almost no chin at all, and — a grotesque accent to this lack — she wears bright red lipstick.

Also alone, at the next table, is a fat young man. His hair is dark because it's unwashed. His sport coat is buttoned up and too small.

Another woman, striking in a man's gray, pin-striped suit that's loose on her slim self, gets up from a stool at the counter by the kitchen and carries her coffee to the fat man's table.

"You're in my class," she says.

The fat man winces, a furtive glance at the attractive woman before him. He expects ridicule. From everyone.

"You sit behind me," she says.

The fat man mutters, "In history."

"Exactly." The pretty woman sits down across from the fat man. "Is it okay if I sit with you?"

He barely nods. With one inexplicable and jerky motion, he nearly knocks over the open ketchup bottle set beside his French fries. A quick look around the café, a scan for the giggling sorority sisters or the smirking boyfriend who sent this woman to his table.

"I like your sport coat," she says. "I wish more of the guys on campus dressed as nice as you do. You look collegiate." She gives the fat man a chance to return the compliment, like anyone would know to do, or at least to say thank you.

She says, "As you can see, I like to dress up too." She tugs at the lapels of her coat. Beneath the coat, she wears a pink shirt, the uppermost buttons undone. His eyes linger on her breasts for too long, drawn to them by her gesture. He knows he's lingering too long. He finally makes eye contact. Her eyes are very green. He doesn't know it, but she's wearing colored contact lenses. She looks at his plate.

Finally, he acts as he ought and pushes his French fries toward her. "Have some," he blurts, too loud.

She takes a fry. She eats it quickly, then takes another. She's through five fries before she points at him — with a ketchup-dipped fry — and asks, "In class today, what did you think of that story, about the Chinese guy?"

"Wan Ju?"

"Yeah." She eats another fry. The fat man is vaguely grateful. "Do you believe it?"

"I like to," he says.

She nods, fervently. "Me too! Me too."

Finally, the woman with the weak chin leans over. She's perturbed.

"I'm in that class too," she says. "I sit in the back row. And every day I watch this loser carefully lifting strands of your hair from your shoulders and sniffing at them and studying them during class." She looks at the fat man. "It's disgusting. You are disgusting."

The fat man is horrified because he does collect strands of hair from the pretty woman's jacket during class, and he does sniff them, and look at them in the morning sunlight. He stares aghast at the woman with the green jacket and turns to face the woman seated across from him.

She leans across the table and smiles. She turns to the woman with the green jacket and says, "Why don't you just go and grow a chin?"

[PLATE 39]

"M. Boileau at the Café"

1893, 31½ x 25⅝

Again, absinthe is the light in the room. Boileau leans back, afraid of illumination. Dominoes lie flat on the table. Boileau has learned through years of experience as a journalist that no one wants to know what you think.

M. Boileau discovered that when he walked, he walked into the future. He said, "I do not wish to go far," and he said, "I don't know if I advance time or skip over time."

"Uh-huh," I said.

M. Boileau was a hypochondriac. "The future" was only his latest "ailment." I told him, time and again, if he would just lose some weight, smoke only before exercising and after dinner (cigarette and cigar or pipe, respectively), and quit the liqueur for cognac, brandy, or — if you must! — port or sherry. He was a dreadful patient.

A friend, though, indeed, even when caught in an apoplectic fit of fancy. One of the few who could raise my spirits enough to face my wife, who could not forgive me for our son's illness. My household cooled fast upon my arrival, I could feel the warmth leave, knew it was there only when I was not, and I tried not to be there, more and more often.

Boileau was a newspaperman. Many of his ailments were the result of the stories he wrote. He observed foul trends.

"At first," Boileau said, "I walked from my favorite chair to my humidor — for my health, on your recommendation, I smoke a cigar in the evening."

"Ah."

"Before I could retrieve a cigar, I found myself transported to the next morning."

"And when you did, did your head feel like rubber? Could you barely stomach a slice of toast?"

Indignantly, Boileau puffed his cigarette. He puffed, "I was not drunk. So. In my chair, dear friend — " his endearments were sincere and never failed to please me — "I was enjoying composing a review in my head, as I often do, conducting the words while free in the air, before a keystroke is struck, when I lost the thread of my thoughts. The thread — it slipped away — for a time I watched as it grew distant. Once the thread was gone, I was lost in thought, actually lost, with no tether. That is when I stood up and walked to the humidor, only to find myself, seconds later, in the middle of the next morning."

"Boileau."

"Listen a little more. I watched myself come down the stairs, in slippers and robe. I hid behind my own chair, in my own home — from myself. Am I really that fat?"

"Oh no, hardly, not at all."

He leaned back. He really was quite fat.

"How did I return, you wonder?"

"Ah! The rest of your story."

"Thinking I must have fallen asleep — hoping — I closed my eyes and there saw the thread. I moved toward it, followed it back, word by word, into my chair."

"That's very clever," I said. "I did not know you were so clever."

"Mm. Listen. The next morning, as I came down the stairs in my robe and slippers,

I caught a glimpse of myself hiding behind my chair — a quick enough glimpse, I could dismiss it as a flicker of sunlight, until later, when I remembered I had been in this moment before, hidden behind my chair, as I climbed down my stairs."

I could not resist teasing my friend. "Tell me, Boileau, what stocks should I buy?"

"Even though you don't believe my story, I'd like to tell the rest of it."

"Of course, of course."

Boileau was too intent on his weird tale to ask me how I was, and that was good. Earlier that evening, when I returned home from work, my wife and I argued. My son's condition, worse.

"At the breakfast table, I lost the thread of my thoughts once again, only this time I walked all the way to the office. And so I saw a future so far-flung, I hardly recognized our city. I hardly knew that I was, in fact, standing where my office is now but in the future where it once was. I stood calf deep in putrid water — wearing these very pants, my friend." He pushed back from our table. He tried, but could not raise his leg high enough for me to see, so I stood, and sure enough, his pants were stained. "I stood in water to my calves but I could see from the stained brick that the waters had been much higher.

"With little thought except to get out of the water — the smell all around was dreadful — I entered the building that is now my office but then was something else, and, presumably because of the flood, devoid of people.

"Except, I found, to my horror." He stopped, just like that, and reached for his drink. He'd not pulled his chair back under the table and seemed too drained to do so, so I pushed his drink to the edge of the table. He thanked me, drank, lit a cigarette, offered me one which I declined, though I wanted it, and drank some more. "I'm sorry, friend. I wasn't prepared then and am not now. Corpses, ten or more, mostly elderly women, all huddled together in the attic. I thought perhaps they'd drowned, but the attic was bone dry, and there was no trace of flood damage. I didn't figure it out until moments before you showed up." Boileau leaned forward and said, "They starved to death. Trapped by the flood."

This was the sort of grim story Boileau wrote, and he'd shared with me plenty, but he never believed his own symptoms, he never believed that mankind was evil, even when he told me about the ghosts who lynched young black men, about the father who chummed the bay with his invalid son, about suicide, upon suicide, upon suicide.

His disbelief was the reason I would not tell him about my boy, bedridden, ill with something he caught at a brothel. I'm not sure Boileau would understand that no wife should ever question her husband, let alone shut him out of her bedroom, out of his son's life, or put an ice-cold pall over his home. I introduced my son to women as my father had introduced me. Every rite has its sacrifices.

Boileau said, "I did find my way back, with the thread of my words, and I stood before my office building as it is today, bricks dry as bone, and I felt violently ill. My friend, God will break his covenant. God will ignore the rainbow seal and will flood the world again. After I saw those old women's corpses I wondered: when the second flood comes, will God give man the time to build another ark?"

"Oh, Boileau," I replied. "Why are you so upset? How did you stain your pant legs?" I knew Boileau was lying about the future, because I dreamed of the future, and it was not as he described. After Boileau dies, after I do, and after our children die, and—perhaps—their children, there is nothing.

[PLATE 40]

"At the Moulin de la Galette"

1890, 35³/₈ x 39³/₈

Here, the woman with the green face appears for the first time; we see her again in At the Moulin Rouge. *The crowd, dancers, and onlookers alike appear to fall toward a gloomy corner of the nightclub: a corner is a vanishing point. Even the little saucers in the foreground tilt toward that black hole.*

At the Moulin de la Galette, a little club on the third floor of a soot-blackened brick building, hidden beneath the elevated rail, Thursday night is British Re-invasion night, known to usual attendees as "Model," as in, "Are you going to Model tonight?" Most dress like black and white pills, like film footage from 1964.

So the redhead in the strawberry summer dress stood out, vibrant.

Her escort, the boy, went often and dressed it: black jeans, black jacket, white shirt, skinny black tie. Sunglasses in his shirt pocket. Most bought secondhand. At the door, they carded the couple. The boy carried his ID and the redhead's. She wore no pockets.

◆ ◆ ◆

The ground floor of the soot-blackened building was occupied by a bar. Every night was the same. The regulars at the bar all worked at the nearby sports arena. The bar, dartboard, counter-top jukeboxes, Budweiser clock. A woman seated with her back to the bar watched the boy and the redhead get their hands stamped for Model. The woman and the redhead caught eyes — the woman, in her thirties, her tight and unflattering jeans, her hair sprayed high; the redhead, her dress, diaphanous, lit by neon, her body, her youth.

✦ ✦ ✦

The boy pointed up the stairs, an "after you" gesture; the redhead was sure his eyes were on her bare legs and her *derrière,* as she thought of it, hoped so, that he might even get a glimpse of her panties, which she'd worn especially for him, pale blue and see-through. He called her out of the blue. Or, rather, she learned, he and his girlfriend just broke up.

The redhead wished he'd told her what people wore to Model, the girls here were all done up like Pan Am flight attendants and Brigitte Bardot. Ah well, she'd be Dorothy.

"There aren't too many people here," she said.

The boy didn't look at the redhead when he told her, "We're early," but looked to her when he added, "You have to come early." He looked to the bar and said, "Let me buy you a drink." She nodded and stood where he left her, a mile from the bar and a mile from the dance floor and somewhere within a mile of a small, worn-out pool table, where stood two girls, not really playing. The boy returned with a Cosmopolitan, not at all what the redhead wanted. Martinis hobble: she could not move easily without a spill. She sipped. "What are you drinking?" she asked. "Scotch and Coke." Scotch and Coke? Her next drink would be clear and in a tumbler.

✦ ✦ ✦

The girls at the pool table were Camille and Marguerite and went to Model every week. The redhead knew they didn't like her when she said, "This club seems pretty neat," and Camille shrugged and Marguerite said, "It's getting old."

They knew that the boy was freshly single and touched his arms and leaned against him and leaned across the table more than was necessary. Camille wore tight, dark-blue jeans, waist well above her bellybutton, and a little white blouse. Marguerite wore a black and white polka-dot dress, black stockings, and very high heels. Her face was green — the light? Make-up?

The redhead kissed the boy on the corner of his mouth — meant to plant a kiss full-on, but missed when he turned to look at something — his drink, the rising hem of Marguerite's dress as she draped herself across the pool table to make a simple shot, the cracked window that let in a harsh beam of a streetlight. The redhead waited and waited and when the boy looked at her at last she sucked the maraschino cherry out of her empty martini glass, stem and all. Camille rolled her eyes but the boy was interested.

She tied the stem into a knot with her tongue.

"You'll excuse me," she said, but before she left to go to the bar she delicately removed the stem from her mouth and placed it in the boy's open palm.

✦ ✦ ✦

At the bar — the club was crowded now — the DJ spun whole albums — the redhead waited. A boy in a gray suit asked, "Can I buy you a drink?"

"You can."

"What do you drink?"

"Vodka tonic."

"Don't you want something sweet?"

"Sure I do. But not to drink."

She could get away with such corny lines, especially while she wore her strawberry dress, especially when she pouted the lines out, tilted her head down but looked up, she didn't need fake eyelashes, she didn't need Cleopatra eyeliner, she was *a lovely thing,* that's how she thought of herself, her eyes, her mouth, her whole petite body always just on the verge of tears, *wracked with tears,* which absolutely melted most boys.

Even, she was sure, the boy.

The boy in the gray suit was surprised by how quickly the redhead's drink disappeared into her little self but he saw this as potentially a good sign, so he ponied up the dough for a second drink. She ordered not another vodka tonic. "I want a Rusty Nail." The bartender looked up the recipe. Drambuie? Hidden behind more popular liqueurs, opened long ago, dusty, sticky.

The boy in the gray suit asked, "Do you want to dance?"

"Sure."

The redhead held her drink high, slipped through the crowd to the dance floor, moved like she didn't care. The boy in the gray suit danced like a Model usual, a mix of old styles. David Bowie? Oh sure, the "Hammer & Sickle." Monkees? "The Twist." The Smiths, boo hoo, the "Bitter-Malt." Beatles, thank the Lord in all His great wisdom, "The Bash." Etc.

The redhead led the boy in the gray suit to a spot where the boy, who stood in a corner and was obviously trying to hide the fact that he was girl-less and wondering where his date got off to, could watch.

✦ ✦ ✦

Camille and Marguerite put on a show. Camille draped a leg across Marguerite's lap. Marguerite ran a finger from the little blue bow on Camille's shoe all the way up to Camille's thigh. Camille sipped a Sidecar. Marguerite kissed Camille's cheek and both girls giggled. Boys brought drinks.

The boy barely danced, twisted around to see Camille and Marguerite.

The redhead put a hand to his cheek, to keep the boy's eyes on her, and said, "They are so phony. I can't believe anyone would fall for that."

A crowd of boys.

"Get me a drink," she said to the boy.

The boy nodded, slow like he was sleepy, started to the bar but the redhead grabbed his arm: "Get me a Rusty Nail. That's what I'm drinking. And hurry back. That guy in the suit is bothering me." This worked, and the boy regained some focus.

✦ ✦ ✦

The boy was confused. His girlfriend dumped him. He hoped she might show at Model. He invited the redhead because he knew she would say yes and because she was beautiful. She made him nervous. As did Marguerite, who seemed . . . interested. All this was titillating and he accepted that he wanted to take things as far as he could without becoming . . . obliged.

A Rusty Nail? Sure. A Rusty Nail.

✦ ✦ ✦

Camille and Marguerite told the boy about an after-hours party at the DJ's apartment. The redhead was very drunk; she told the boy in the gray suit that he was, "only a silly fool," that she was with somebody, couldn't he see that, and that, "she was really flattered," but she inflected "flattered" so it stung like a slap in the face. The boy retrieved the redhead, unaware that there even was a boy in a gray suit. "There's a party, do you want to go?" the boy asked the redhead.

"A party. How lovely!" She spoke too loudly, now that the lights were up and the music off. "Will there be alcohol?" she asked. She poked the boy in the chest, "I don't think I should drink anymore."

"We're going to share cabs," Marguerite informed the boy. She lit a cigarette. A bouncer told her she couldn't smoke. She flipped him the bird and they both laughed.

✦ ✦ ✦

The bar downstairs was empty.

✦ ✦ ✦

Outside, on the sidewalk in front of the club, Camille, Marguerite, and the boy talked about how Model had gone to shit. Cabs waited, lurked beneath the elevated rail.

The redhead sat down hard on the curb. She sat with her knees up, her panties exposed. The boy saw blue, see-through. He crouched down and held the redhead's knees together. "Get up," he said. "We're going to share a cab."

"You have my money anyhow," she said. "You don't need me."

"Come with me to this party."

"Why did you take me to this place, if you hate it so much?"

The boy sat down on the curb beside the redhead.

Camille and Marguerite waved a cab over. "Are you coming?" they asked.

The redhead said, "I'm humiliated. I'm not dressed right. Why don't you love me? You only call me when one of your girlfriends leaves you. You're so cruel to me and I only love you." She rested her head against the boy's shoulder. He put his arm around her and she shrugged it off.

Camille and Marguerite didn't wait.

I am cruel, he thought, and he grinned. He put his arm around her and said, "Get up. We'll walk together through the city. It's warm tonight. I am cruel."

[PLATE 41]

"A La Mie"

1891, 19 ¾ x 27 ½

Upon seeing this painting, Degas made a bad pun: "A la me, a la you." I admit I laughed. I never got his next joke: "These crumbs are the dregs." The two in this portrait were friends of Toulouse-Lautrec's. He called the painting, "The Schemers." Note the candy stripes — Toulouse-Lautrec loved to repeat motifs because every object has more than one meaning.

We're hunched over a little table in the café where we've eaten; we've left rind, orange, and wax. We still have port in our glasses. We're tired of our lives. Like all who pass our table, all who eat and eat and eat. We know, as all do in their hearts, the solution is money.

But we did not want money, because we were not interested. We were interested in this question that occurred to us: What could we do that would delight?

"There is a local story . . ."

"Yes?"

"About a bird . . ."

"Mmm-hmm."

"That pecked at the sky and brought in its beak bits of it."

"For its chicks?"

"For the townspeople."

"Was this day sky or night sky?"

"There is no sky at night. Or maybe the sky is invisible at night? Maybe the moon hides it? Your question is a silly question. The sky is blue."

"Oh. So. What did the townspeople do with their bits of blue sky?"

"You know how beautiful the sky is. At various heights, all kinds of blue. People had sky cut and set, people made goblets, bowls, vases. Lenses for eyeglasses. One boy was given a little whale made of thick, pre-dawn sky and he hung it at his window."

"That is delightful. Yes! So, do we capture the bird?"

"Capture the bird?"

"To collect the sky with which we can delight people."

"I don't think so."

"We collect the sky ourselves? I have a post-hole digger in the truck."

"No, no. This is only a local story. A legend. I don't believe it's true. Just . . . delightful. Yes. Delightful."

"How then, does it help us?"

"An example. An example only. Should we order more port?"

Our glasses were empty.

"I'd say probably not."

We ordered more port.

"Blue lenses, really?"

"Yes."

"I would like that. I would like to see the world like that."

"Must be what it's like in the ocean. The warm oceans, where the water is clear and you can see everything, and hear the songs whales make. Hold on. In such blue seas, if whales are blue, how can you see them?"

"I don't think whales are blue."

We drank a little more.

"Would you look at that."

"At what?"

"Over there. A baby. A young mother. Look. The baby claps."

"And the mother, too, encouraging her daughter."

"So sweet, really."

"The baby . . ."

"Yes?"

"In our direction."

"Oh, yes."

"Perhaps . . . perhaps if we smile . . ."

We smile for the baby.

[PLATE 42]

"La Goulue Entering the Moulin Rouge"
1892, 31½ x 23

La Goulue is "The Glutton." Toulouse-Lautrec's bizarre presentation gives her a certain sinister grandeur. His most spectacular portraits, like this one, have a way of summoning up the portraiture of Goya, who lurked behind Manet, who stood over and beside Degas, who was my mentor.

In a desert is a hotel called el Greco. When the temperature at noon is in the hundreds, the nights are still cold. The owners of the hotel view el Greco as an albatross, a mirage only to be found by those who are lost. The rail line that once passed near the hotel, long since dead. So, the owners do not care who we are, so long as our checks clear. They cash our checks, drawn against banks they've never heard of, banks they guess must be European but are not European; our banks are a part of the world's secret economy.

Madame Goulue's voice is always at my ear, even if only as a sliver of bone.

We rent el Greco for The Ball.

Once a year, toward the middle of the summer when the heat is so great it's exotic, we rent el Greco for The Ball. The wood of the hotel is so dry, it crackles like fire when the wind blows. We go to The Ball as we are; we is me, Madame Goulue, and Goulue's hermaphrodite, whom I call Glynn, and we is the rest of us. Others come too, every year, newcomers. There are always newcomers. Newcomers wear costumes, as is the rule, and they must observe the rules. Newcomers' costumes are often marvelous, made of rubber tubing and foam, bicycle parts and the guts of old computers. The least imaginative come dressed as traffic accidents. We come as we are, but our appearance is so traditional, it's bizarre, and so, as far as the newcomers are concerned, we are in costume too.

Several days before The Ball, a village is erected by the newcomers. We walk among the tents and desert vehicles as if we, too, were newcomers. Undetected. The newcomers chant and draw and listen for the train that doesn't come, hasn't come, came only long ago. Late, late, the whistle blows.

We only make ourselves known on the night of The Ball.

The temperature drops, nearly sixty degrees.

Glynn holds onto Madame Goulue's left arm. Glynn is massive, taller than Goulue and me. Glynn looks about, sternly. Glynn does not dance. I am exquisite. My dress is modest and black, and I wear a wide-brimmed hat, topped with a stuffed thrush, rust-and-blueberry-colored, its eyes replaced with blue stones. All watch me closely, wait for Goulue to release me so they might ask me to dance, approach us because of me, speak with Goulue, timidly, for the opportunity to glance at me.

I am, humbly, Madame Goulue's servant.

Madame Goulue is so pale, the run of her veins can be seen beneath her skin. Her mouth is wide. She wears a smirk of glum lipstick. Her hair is mouse-brown; she wears it double-parted, leaving enough for a plume atop her head. Goulue's dress is the color of the Fourth Horse. The material of the dress is thin; her shrunken breasts are clearly visible; she is otherwise covered by a black slip. Pinned at the neckline is a sprig of a plant that does not grow locally. At her throat is a black ribbon.

As The Ball progresses, the music becomes less and less modern.

Newcomers are expected to behave according to the rules of The Ball, which amount to one rule, which is respect the organizers of The Ball. Those newcomers who do not, do not return the next year. We offer guidance and reprimand for those who are inexperienced.

I dance until I see Madame Goulue is back on the floor, fully vivified, and without her black ribbon. No longer does she require the support of Glynn, who skulks at the edge of the dance floor. I leave the ballroom, and climb the stairs. Our room is on the top floor, at the back of the hotel. Once in our room, I undress; I work naked. My work is vigorous and I work vigorously. The newcomer wears Goulue's ribbon around his neck. I untie the ribbon and wash it in the sink. When the ribbon is clean, and draped over the headboard, I begin to dismember what is left of the newcomer.

Already, the dry wood of el Greco has absorbed the stain and the spatter.

[PLATE 43]

"At the Moulin Rouge"

1892, 47 ½ x 55 ¼

Now the woman with the green face asserts herself more fully. Though at the margins, she looks directly at you. Passing behind, the whiff of a thought, is Toulouse-Lautrec himself. The walls are the color of oxidized copper. Look at her face, says Toulouse-Lautrec; at her face, said Degas.

Our deaths came sooner than any of us imagined they would. Sure, we imagined our deaths. We did so because we were young. None of us believed we were immortal; we only believed that death would not dare an untimely visit. Once, Gabriel did say, "We don't know if we're not immortal for sure until we die," but he always was one to articulate worthless truths.

Halloween is a good day to imagine your death, but when we were in our young twenties, we did not think so. Halloween meant to us a night full of parties, meant the girls we most desired to see naked went out practically so, meant pleasure, every-where, all night. The trains we rode to work everyday were fun, all the shops were decorated to draw on our nostalgia even as we lived in the moment, we could drink, ask what we would not ask out of costume, sleep with strangers, with virtual strang-ers, with those whom we loved but never had the courage to invite.

We were five friends. Before the first party, we agreed to meet at our favorite diner. All in costume, and, by coincidence, all with our faces painted to look like skulls, to honor the skulls beneath our skin and muscle and fat. I suppose, by doing so, we managed to mark ourselves. Two of us died that night.

At the door my waitress, the waitress who flirted back and sat on the bench beside me when I ordered, she said, "Boo," and when I asked if I could pick her up when her shift was over — a question I never dared to ask before — she said, "Sure." Her face was painted green, a corpse less progressed than ours which were bone.

We all wore secondhand suits and dresses and at the long table in the back we plotted our night, party to party. Later, I would meet my waitress. She and I would go to the last parties, those that ended just before the sun rose and the birds went crazy. Thousands of ravens in one tree turned the tree black.

None of our deaths were extraordinary. A knot of malignant cells photographed in the brain, an inefficient heart, earlier than anyone expected. When we died, in the days surrounding our deaths, death seemed extraordinary, but it was not and showed itself to be ordinary. We saw it was ordinary when we died, when those we knew died, and when the millions we did not know died.

My waitress joked with all of us. We all ordered pancakes, heaped the table with plates of pancakes and bowls of applesauce. We drank autumnal beers. Our meal was better for anticipation. The walls of the diner shone green and brown. My waitress leaned against me, rested a hand on my shoulder while she asked if everyone had what they wanted.

Was I in love? I was not sure, then. Yes, I was in love. At the parties, I waited for her shift to end. No matter how lovely the angel, the black cat, the French maid, nothing would happen until her shift ended. I called her my waitress, my friends, "your waitress," but she was only her own. She did not need because she was. Which makes it doubtful she was in love with me. Outside, trees and the breeze, a moment of quiet before more costumes showed up, or took off, or stepped outside for a smoke.

My waitress and I died that night. I drove to the diner to meet her, to take her to the last Halloween parties of the year. On the roadway that runs alongside the river, my car spun out on a patch of ice, slipped across a narrow band of frozen grass, and into the water. As the car sank, I saw city lights. The lights that lined the bridge and the great, rippling neon sign that promoted a brand of gasoline. She saw my face: a bright white skull.

[PLATE 44]

"La Visite: Rue des Moulins"

1894, 31³/₄ x 24¹/₄

Two prostitutes lined up for medical inspection, their flimsy dresses held up over their hips, their knickers off. In profile, they look quite different, but if you were to turn your back on them, they would appear quite identical. That is, they would both disappear completely.

She rattled the key, suddenly so obviously an inferior spare, struggled with the padlock that kept the storefront accordion grate shut. "Who lives here?" I asked. The padlock sprang open. Behind the grate was a deadbolt door. "My brother's ex-girlfriend and her boyfriend." "Are they here now?" "I don't know." The deadbolt unlocked, she tried the door (glass but soaped opaque), she yanked and the door scraped open.

"People live here?" I hated my question. She said people lived there. Just because it looked like an abandoned secondhand shop.

"You see that room back there?" she pointed. "That's their bedroom." She called out two names — theirs, presumably. The walls were painted red, each wall a different shade, a range from rose-pink to crimson. The ceiling was gold-painted, pressed tin. Exposed pipes and vents suspended beneath the gold. But all that was background to stuff. Stuff all along the walls, interrupted by a living space — mismatched couches as low walls, then: more stuff, interrupted by a little kitchen, adequate only for cereal making and noodle boiling.

I said, "It's late."

She said, "Pull the grate shut. Lock the door."

I did what she told me. A glance out into the night-world of the city: a broad and empty boulevard, a smattering of streetlamps, a smashed-up parked car, and the high wall of factory buildings. Padlock locked, deadbolt shot; I'd known her since eight that morning and vibrated with infatuation. Which is why I was in an apartment that looked like an abandoned secondhand store and not at the Westin, where a room, paid for by my company, remained vacant.

A man's voice — from the bedroom. "Do you hear that?" I asked.

She looked through a stack of paintings, lifted one, put it to the side, lifted the next, etc.

The voice again — but not in the bedroom. Out on the street. A tiny window in the back of the apartment was open a crack. I crossed the room to close and lock the window.

As I passed her she said, "Look at all these paintings."

Lock threaded, window secured, I asked, "What?"

"These." All of the paintings were unframed canvases on stretchers. She held up two. One of a city, the other of a woman.

"Is that you?" I asked.

She gave the painting a second look. "That doesn't look like me."

In fact, it did, exactly. Younger, but not by much.

"I'm sure that it is you. Who lives here?"

"I told you."

Apprehensively, I opened the bedroom door. Empty. The bed, unmade. Otherwise the room was clean. In contrast to the rest of the place, the bedroom was quite bare. She gave me a look I couldn't decide how to read.

She said, "Are you tired already?"

"Not at all." I closed the bedroom door.

She dropped the paintings and skipped over to the kitchen area. "Let's see," she said. She opened cupboards until, "Aha!" She withdrew a bottle and two glasses. She filled them both to the brim and carried them to the coffee table in the living area. She dropped onto a couch, dust rose up all around her, and her dress rose high on her legs. She crossed her legs and said, "Sit down." I did, and tried a sip of what she'd poured. "What is this?" I asked. "Rum." "Don't you at least want an ice cube?" She shrugged; I fetched some ice. As I opened the freezer, I asked myself why her brother's ex-girlfriend would be so generous . . . before I worried further, she said, "This morning I dreamed about little children."

Two ice cubes for each glass. I sat beside her. My weight on the couch caused her body to tilt toward me, for her shoulder to make contact with mine. This casual touch, then she put her weight against me to tuck her legs up under herself.

"The children were perfectly gorgeous." She leaned forward for her drink and I glanced at the cleavage her doing so exposed. "I became frightened." She shrugged and sat back. "Look at that bruise." She pointed at her thigh where there was an iodine-colored stain, and darker.

"Why did you become frightened?" I asked, gaze held by her bruise, her thigh.

"The children looked perfect, but they weren't. Some kind of dark magic. You know how I got this bruise?"

"No."

"Mechanical bull."

I believed her. I dutifully drank the rum and I enjoyed it more with each sip.

She got up from the couch and I watched, her dress fell around her, swung about her legs, she slipped into a little room I presumed must be the bathroom. Running water. Her rum was almost gone. I didn't look around the apartment at all even though it was filled with things to see. Instead, I kept my eyes on the space she had occupied moments before.

When she emerged from the bathroom, she wore only a slip and her stockings.

"Look what I found in the bathroom." With her hands, she outlined the slip she wore. "I like it," she said. Her stockings were blue. "Don't look so surprised," she said. "Do you wear your whole suit to bed? Take off your tie!" I touched the knot of my tie — a tie I'd stopped being aware of early that morning, soon after she'd said, "This conference is boring. Let's skip the next talk together."

She found a dressmaker's dummy, a cloth torso mounted on a metal post, and stood beside it. The dummy wore a slip, not unlike the one she'd borrowed from the bathroom; the dummy's slip was pinned up, the dummy's hips exposed. "What a funny way to wear your gown," she said to the dummy.

And she lifted her borrowed slip up over her hips. She wore nothing beneath.

And the front gate was opened, the door unlocked.

The couple that stepped inside stood motionless. Me, on their couch, hand still at the knot of my tie; her, nearly naked, wearing a borrowed slip, mimicking a tailor's dummy. Moments later I found out who really lived in the apartment that looked like a secondhand shop, and why he had a painting of the woman I'd met and fallen for that very morning.

[PLATE 45]

"Woman Fixing Her Stocking"

1894, 23 ⅝ x 16 ⅞

A little sketch, of a young prostitute. Her breath, visible on the speckled cardboard: white. Her dress, about her neck, and her stockings: green. He loved her. That is plain. I knew the moment I saw the sketch, found in the room Toulouse-Lautrec kept at the brothel in Albi.

High school. At the end of the school day. She and I worked together on some extra-curricular that wasn't sports. I wore my school uniform haggard, wore it all day, would fall asleep wearing it; those cheap blue pants, one of four white shirts, one of quite a number of ties. She changed out of her uniform. Folded her skirt for jeans. Her shirt for — another blouse. How pretty she was in — whatever. When I would meet her at the movie theater, where she worked, I marveled: gorgeous, in polyester.

One afternoon I walked into the classroom where our after-school meeting was — early, I guess — and caught her mid-change. Blouse up around her shoulders, bent over to pull up one long sock, otherwise naked. Her red hair, caught up in some kind of elastic, though loose. Rather than stumble out an apology and stumble out of the room, rather than squeal and cover herself, I became still and she, too, for a moment. I watched and she put on jeans, pulled her blouse down over her breasts, folded her uniform and said, "I suppose we should wait for everyone else," and "Come, sit next to me." I did and we did.

She gave me an image, that afternoon. What happened after, happened. That she had a crush on me, was. When school was over, we graduated, she and I, together. Summer, together. Then she went away but left behind a moment. Women after her either found that moment —

or didn't.

Years later, maybe in the distant future, maybe in outer space, my wife and I honeymooned in a small museum. Even a small museum can be rich and engrossing. The way a Fabergé egg can take days to examine and just when you think you've seen the whole of it, you locate hinge and latch.

Of course, my wife had found the moment, that image I carried with me; she seemed to find it over and over: right leg bent, toes to the floor; left leg locked; body bent slightly at the waist; focused on the task of pulling up a dark stocking; green-blue blouse around her neck, held up by her shoulders; breasts uncovered, sun bright on her chest; red hair, tied back but tumbled forward. Yet —

My wife — my wife — did something to the image that seemed at times wrong, at least different. This troubled me, but —

When my wife was animated, speaking, sleeping, breathing, lovemaking — she made the image seem less important than it had until she dimly recreated it, the same but — wrong.

She did so on the first night of our honeymoon, late, after we'd spent hours looking at the tiny paintings and drawings in the museum. After, we had salad and salmon and sorbet. We made love in a room that was a recreation of a late century classroom where, after we'd made love, she made that moment, that image, and wrong, somehow: I stood still and she didn't and then I dressed and we went for a late night walk in the dark museum. I tried to ignore that the image/moment I'd carried with me so long was damaged and damaged by my wife, tried to ignore the uncertainty that this made.

But: there in that museum is a study for a greater painting. And that study poured into me a soothing epiphany. I sat on a bench and looked at a painting of fog boiling up from a valley. I contemplated my epiphany. I picture my wife, nearly nude, leaning over to pull up her stocking. Her small breasts, her full hips. I think on this for pleasure. She is all.

[PLATE 46]

"The Grand Loge"

1897, 21¹/₄ x 18¹/₄

Much like myself, Toulouse-Lautrec was as interested in the theatergoer as in the show. The woman who appears to have spotted her observer has a lovely face like a mask, bone white and finely featured. Her eyes are blanks: they are pearls.

A family of four, a father, mother, sister and brother went to see the symphony. The father wore a suit, the mother a dress and the perfume that smells to her husband of romance and to her children of security. The daughter wore a dress, too, that she borrowed from a friend and insisted on wearing and the son was dressed by his parents in corduroy pants, a yellow button-down shirt and a green and navy striped tie.

The son was thrilled with their seats: way up in the highest balcony, set back so he could see the orchestra and almost the entire audience. Across from the family were two women, one slightly older than the other. In the balcony next to theirs was a man.

The orchestra made their final tuning noise, which the son liked the sound of, the conductor raised his hands and dropped them, and the strings came in, slow. The mother kept one eye on the children, and one on the orchestra; the father kept one eye on the orchestra, and one on the mother. He inhaled deeply.

The boy immediately began to work out how he could get to the balcony oppo-site his family's. He tried to work out climbing among the statuary set into the wall and along the metal framework from which lights and microphones were hung. That seemed to get him only so far; his palms were sweaty; in his mind he was out on the metal framework and there was a pretty big gap between him and the balcony, too big to jump. Looking up, he spied one of the many chandeliers and figured that if he could jump up and grab it, he could get it swinging enough to send him into the balcony with the two women.

Then he began to work out why he might need to do this. He threw out fire be-cause then he'd need to save his family. He decided that the younger woman—who had once glanced in his direction and had an angular, pale face that he thought was pretty—was being held captive by the woman sitting next to her, and by the man in the next balcony, the man with the flat face and the nose that hung down like an icicle. To save her, he would climb silently and unnoticed to the chandelier and then swing into the balcony, kicking the older woman and pulling the younger woman to the floor so the man with the flat face couldn't shoot either of them. Then he would determine if they needed to swing their way to freedom, or if they could just take the stairs.

After the intermission, the boy's sister nudged him in the arm with her elbow. He looked over at her and she handed him her program booklet. On the back, where there was plenty of blank space, she had made a drawing. She was a very good artist, and her brother recognized immediately the people she had depicted: the two women in the balcony across the way and the man with the flat face in the balcony one over; also, she'd drawn in her brother, swinging from a chandelier. This startled the brother so much that he gasped and threw the program over the edge of the balcony. The mother put a hand to her forehead and the father looked at the brother and sister sternly, but also with mirth all around his eyes.

[PLATE 47]

"The Toilette"

1896, 25 ⁵/₈ x 20 ⁷/₈

When a light caught his eye, Toulouse-Lautrec borrowed that light freely. This picture is reminiscent of numerous of Degas' nude bathers—and to the good: though Degas became a terrible old man, he left many lights worth borrowing.

My girlfriend sat on the floor naked except for a white sheet bunched around her rear end and pulled over her thighs and a pair of black stockings, which were wrinkled below her knees. Her red hair was knotted at the back of her head. We'd started living together a week ago, after bumping into each other less than a month ago and reminiscing about when we'd known each other in school. We lived in a studio apartment, which was all we could afford, even with the both of us working and splitting the rent. We liked the wood floors and it came furnished with white wicker furniture. We thought the furniture was odd.

She sat very straight. I thought she was holding a yoga position, but she was too still and her face too blank. I needed my shirt for work, but my shirt was draped on the back of a chair in her sight line, and I didn't want to break her concentration, or, if not concentration, her reverie on nothing.

But I had to get dressed. I was nearly late—cutting it close because earlier she'd stopped me from getting dressed so we could make love. Though we were broke and that hung over us all the time, our relationship was still very new and so we were excited all the time, too. I got my shirt.

"Hello," she said.

"Are you okay?" I asked.

"Yes." She smiled up at me. Her skin was pale and her lips were full. I thought she was quite beautiful.

"Are you thinking?"

"Not exactly. Look at the light."

I looked to where she pointed and there was a pattern of sunlight, shaped like an open book, on the wall in front of her, just below one of her easels.

"Mm-hmm," I said. "It's pretty."

"The light caught my eye so I sat here to look at it. While I did I had a daydream."

I looked at her seated cross-legged on the floor. She had small shoulders and small breasts. Her stomach was soft but small and her hips narrow. There was shadow between her legs, where she was clean shaven. I looked back at her face, at her wide eyes. I was incredibly attracted to her, pleased she was my girlfriend, but at the same time she'd done some odd things since we moved in together, things odd in a way that I could find no reference for, no connection with. I decided they were charming.

"What was your daydream about and then I have to go to work."

She rocked forward. She said: "In my daydream I was sitting on the floor just as I am. I was looking at the light on the wall and it was relaxing me. I knew I had to get dressed and get going because you had to go to work and I wanted to walk you to the train and buy a pack of cigarettes. At the same time all I wanted to do was to stay here, right here and stare at the light and relax. I began to feel this tugging, then: a tugging between the me who wanted to be with you and the me who wanted to be with the light."

I looked at the light again, then back at her face. She held her chin high, which exposed her long and pale neck.

"The tugging continued. It wasn't painful, exactly, but like the tug you feel when you're on Novocain and having your teeth pulled. And my skeleton started to come out of me. As if my skin was no denser than thick oatmeal, my skeleton just started to force its way out of me. Once it was completely out it sat in front of me. My skeleton was very friendly looking."

"I would imagine so." I glanced at the clock.

"We looked at each other and somehow it was decided that my skeleton would go with you to the train and get some cigarettes and come back. So, you and the skeleton went out, arm in arm just as if it were you and me going out the door. I stayed behind and looked at the light."

"Strange," I said.

"But darling, that's not all. I looked at the light and it grew cold in front of me. The light became harsh and my meditation was done for and I had an epiphany: *of course*, I thought. *The soul is in the bones.*"

I didn't know what to say. But she was smiling and so pretty, I didn't worry. I reached into my pocket and took out my cigarettes. "Here," I said. "Have one of mine." She stood up and the sheet fell away. She took the cigarette, put it in her mouth and waited for me to light it. After I did she said, "You just wait a second. Let me throw on some clothes and I'll walk you."

[PLATE 48]

"Madame Berthe Bady"

1897, 27 ⅛ x 22 ⅞

All the movement in this portrait comes not from the figure nor from the brush, but from this painting's disintegration. That Toulouse-Lautrec's hand triggered such rot is a sure sign of his genius.

At sixty, Berthe Bady became paralyzed. Not as the result of a terrible accident, or as the result of an illness *per se*. She froze—lovely, pale hand thoughtfully to her chin—from a lack of satisfaction, an accumulation of letdowns and foiled desires that, over time, had gathered in her joints, permeated her whole skeleton. At sixty, her bones were not brittle but iron.

Her smile, now permanent, expressed many complex feelings and was the cause of much debate. Her smile is, "I know what's coming"; her smile is, "I love to acquiesce"; her smile is, "On the verge of tears"; and so on.

Berthe Bady is much beloved by the people in her neighborhood, a small community in a large city. During the years she was mobile, she only rarely left her little enclave. She knew and was known by shopkeepers, ministers, politicians, boys and men who loved or wanted her, and by women who were never quite her friends because she was quiet and other. Once unable to move, Berthe Bady was tended to by those people, cleaned and dressed and fed.

If curious about specifics, you are bound to be disappointed. The only detail regarding her care that I am privy to is the peculiarity of her stomach, which allows her to be fed. The first morning her clothes were changed it was discovered that there was a door on Berthe Bady's stomach, like the door on a wood stove. Food, arranged with care on a plate, is placed inside her stomach. A mysterious apparatus eats, then the dish is removed. Whether or not Berthe Bady always had a door on her stomach or if the door appeared after her paralysis is not known to me.

That I know even that small detail is the result of a slip made by one of her neighbors, who mistook me for a local. She was not paying attention to me, just thinking out loud as the parade approached.

An annual parade celebrates the extraordinary case of Berthe Bady, which is that neighborhood's proudest achievement. On the last float, upon a green chair, dressed in a lovely black dress, with curtains hung behind her, she rode. All she passes cheer. I only stumbled upon the parade by coincidence.

I'd come looking for Berthe Bady who I'd disappointed many years before. My wife left me. Out of self-pity and loneliness, the image of Berthe Bady came, an image as solid and unchanging as Berthe Bady had indeed become.

That I would attempt to steal her from the horror-parade was fate. The instant her float passed me, I knew I must try. And try I did. But fail I did too. Berthe Bady's neighbors, desperate and insane, carried me off to their prison, where I am now and have been for a very long time, a place I think must be like the inside of Berthe Bady's stomach. And here I will be eaten, by mysterious apparatus.

[PLATE 49]

"Private Room at 'Le Rat Mort'"

1899, 21³/₄ x 18¹/₈

A mixture invented by Toulouse-Lautrec, he prepared his canvas with absinthe and cognac, the former perhaps the source of the green so prevalent in his work? I wonder. Perhaps the fumes from this concoction sent him to the sanatorium. He painted the woman in the private room with all the anger of a washout who still remembers the casual way he once shared his talent.

Aunt Jane was not my aunt but a friend of my father's. The year that I was eight, my mother and father passed me around to all sorts of people while they worked on the details of their divorce. Dad took me to a hotel in the city. Aunt Jane met us in the lobby. She was very happy to see me and kissed my father. He didn't want to leave and said so, and said that he'd be back to get me. Aunt Jane's hat, probably very ugly, was the most beautiful hat I'd ever seen and I said so. She laughed. A tent of veil, twisted like a wax candy wrapper, finished with a black bow.

Back then you could smoke anywhere you pleased and she did. She told me never to smoke. She showed me how to light a cigarette and the first cigarette I ever had came from her purse. "Are you ready for dinner?" she asked and took me to a restaurant inside the hotel. When the maître d' told Aunt Jane the restaurant was very crowded she said, "We're very small so we don't need to wait." We didn't. The maître d' found space for us at the end of a very large booth in a private room. Deep in their dinner conversation, the family already in the booth grew quiet when we sat down.

I said, "Aunt Jane, he sat us with someone else's family."

"No, dear. Tonight we're part of their family."

Everyone at the booth was charmed and chuckled.

"Jane," my mother reminded me whenever I mentioned her, "is not your aunt." After a while, I decided not to tell my mother stories about Aunt Jane.

Aunt Jane ordered a steak and told the waiter just how I wanted my peanut butter sandwich prepared. While we waited for our food the family we'd joined got up to leave. One of the women was pregnant. "She's about to pop," Aunt Jane said.

We ate and I watched Aunt Jane's cigarette with amazement, watched as she let the worm of ash grow an inch long before tapping it into the ashtray and she told me about meeting my father when he was very young and about dresses she wore and, finally, she began to tell me about all the dresses she wanted to get for me and the places she wanted to take me, little shops and marketplaces all over the country, and some out of the country, in foreign cities about which Aunt Jane whispered.

All this excited me terribly. When my father came to pick me up at Aunt Jane's hotel room, I talked and talked, on and on, even when Aunt Jane and my father went into the hall to say goodnight, and I kept on talking all the way home. My father did not once interrupt me and he did not ask me to stop. He only smiled and drove me home to mother's.

Once in bed—"Please stop all your chattering and calm down or you'll never go to sleep," my mother said—once in bed my mind whirled. At times I thought I was awake but was dreaming, at times I was awake but could not be sure—the lights on the walls and ceiling of my bedroom were so lovely, not as I'd ever seen them before. And during that night I had what I think of as a vision.

My mother was pregnant with me. She and Aunt Jane and my father were sitting in the backyard of the house where I used to live with my parents. The sun cast a soft green light in spots across the grass. Aunt Jane and my mother and father were laughing. My father had a glass of lemonade that I knew was so sweet I would not have been able to bear even the tiniest sip. My mother leaned close to my father and kissed him, a gentle kiss on the mouth, and I, the child inside of my mother, emerged from her mouth and crept into my father's. Aunt Jane stood, approached my parents, and with one hand on my mother's shoulder, she kissed my father, and I was in Aunt Jane's mouth. She did not swallow; I worked my way into Aunt Jane, and once I was nestled inside of her, she was pregnant and my mother was not. All this sharing of me was quite jolly. Just before the vision dispersed—fell apart to reveal roving lights on my bedroom wall and then sleep, deep and unilluminated—my mother was my mother again, and the glass of lemonade was drunk.

[PLATE 50]

"The Modiste"

1900, 24 x 19

Toulouse-Lautrec lived a year into the new century. He'd already come apart. He worked to the last, but the faces in his final pictures are all pity. Pity was now all he could muster with a brush.

Husband and wife, on the cusp of their sixties, attend a Saturday reading. A poet friend asked that they come. The reading is at a little bar in a neighborhood neither wife nor husband have been to. After the reading they wander together along the brick sidewalks under dark green ginkgo trees. They decide they'll dine in the neighborhood — at a little restaurant with white lights strung up around the windows. Sun falls on the brick walk in tree patterns: light from a crowd of leaves.

At the end of the street is a small shop, its display window cluttered with trinkets. The husband notices a toy he used to play with, and his eyes grow wide when he comprehends the price tag.

The dark shop is packed with merchandise. The husband walks to the back to look at more old toys, still in their original packages. The wife stops at a waist-high glass case, eye caught by a fur coat. "Real fur," she says to herself. She runs her hand over the coat, lets her thoughts wander; for a moment, she gazes vacantly. She puts the coat to one side, and looks down into the case. Among costume jewelry and keys on rings with hotel names, is a box that strikes her fancy. "Hello," she says. The husband turns around and an elderly man appears from behind a wardrobe. The husband resumes his train of thought: "I always wanted this toy, should I buy it now?" The elderly man takes the box from the case for the wife. "It's a nice one," he says. The box is heavier than she expects and she says so. The elderly man says, "There are smaller boxes inside." She buys the box. Her husband doesn't buy the toy.

At home, while the husband makes a pot of tea, the wife puts the box on the kitchen table. A raised pattern of vines and flowers decorate its metal surface. The box is the size of a grapefruit. She thinks it's pewter. Around the box's middle is a seam; on one side, a hinge. She opens the box and inside is another box.

"Isn't this lovely," she says.

The husband carries the pot of tea to the table. "Did you know?"

"The clerk said there were quite a few inside."

She removes the second box. It rattles. She removes the third box and a fourth. The fourth has no hinge; it's just a cube of metal. "If there is something else, it's sealed in," she says.

"The end," the husband says. He pours out two cups of tea.

Later that night the wife lies wide awake and listens to her husband breathe. She's usually asleep long before her husband. His breathing rattles, boarders on snoring. A line of clean white light — as thin as the seam of a hinged box — razors across the gray comforter. She has the nervous thought that nothing new is ever going to happen, that there will be no more surprises now that the children are out of the house and she and her husband have fallen into a simple — albeit pleasant — routine. Life is not without stimulation, but is without exuberant newness.

She gets out of bed. Downstairs she heats a cup of milk in a saucepan. She eats a spoonful of frozen yogurt from the carton: stands by the open freezer door, uses a dirty teaspoon. She sits at the kitchen table with her milk. The littlest box, the last box, is on the table where she left it. She leans back in her chair. Some bend of the light, some new shadow cast, reveals a seam on the little box—"Not the last box," she thinks. With a little wiggling, she's able to pull the box apart. Inside, another box. This box is shinier than the others. "No one has found this." She's so excited, she gets up to get her husband. She changes her mind, sits down. She pulls at this smallest box and it, too, opens. She opens another box and another. She finds, finally, a box no larger than a tack-head. She attempts to open it; her fingers are too large. She drops the box. Picks it up, fumbles it, drops the box. She puts the tiny box next to all its brothers and looks at it. With the right tools, she could take that little box apart. She'll get the toolbox later. She turns off the kitchen light. Moonlight comes in through the little window over the sink, a ribbon across the table, the little boxes. She rests her head on the table and gazes at the boxes. As she falls asleep she mutters, "That was delicious."

book four
MARY CASSATT

[PLATE 51]

"Head of a Young Girl"

1876, 12¾ x 9

The Salon-rejected "Head of a Young Girl" was undisciplined. The brushwork left too much light on the canvas. My masters were Manet, Courbet, and Degas. I despised conventional art. I began to live.

From an aperture she has made in the Venetian blinds she watches leaves fall. The leaves are white and gold. The leaves are ice-blue and brown and steadily fall. Rain mists, the leaves shine as they fall. The leaves flicker silver. As the leaves fall—so many, they are a wall—she sees herself. Her eye to the windowpane, her self in the wet, falling leaves.

{My beloved husband is a voyeur. A marriage vow: I must become a voyeur also. For a time I watched what he watched and with his eyes. I began with my own self—as our love began, with his gaze upon me. He came to my sister's dinner party as a guest of a guest. He singled me out with his sight and looked at me often. With senses other than sight (all I really had, then), I knew I wanted him and so urged him to look at me, moved into his line of sight whenever possible. I served myself. Dish of squash in hand, I stretched across the table; with a water pitcher I leaned forward and poured. I didn't think then I was beautiful and wouldn't say I think so now.}

As much as she wants to see every leaf at once, she can only see the wall all the leaves make together. The optical illusion of leaves moving made by a single image followed quickly by another single image and then quickly by another. She believes she learned to be a voyeur to know her husband better. In truth, she is a voyeur.

She resisted one of her marriage vows: to lust as her husband lusts. She resists passion. As she looks she puts distance between herself and what she sees. As if the longer she looks the more panes of glass form between her and the object of her gaze. Layers of glass like stacked microscope slides. Her eyes repel light.

{I looked sideways into mirrors, double-mirrors, saw the small of my back, a flick of my long hair. Caught warped glimpses in dinnerware I kept highly polished. The hem of my skirt as it crept and bent, the bulge of an untailored collar at the back of my neck, tag up, caressing the invisible hairs at my nape. I watched myself dress for work, undress, undress, nude. I have seen so much of myself without thinking about what it is I see other than that I must keep seeing and when first I detected that need I knew I'd become as my beloved husband.}

She sees her self in the leaves. She sees her eye in the glittering leaves. Without opening the blinds further she is wholly reproduced by the leaves. A reflection. Head of a young woman. Then bust, then body.

{I learned not to primp too much, not to alter the allure of accident. What arouses my eye is the clot of lipstick on my lower lip, the wile of hair snuck out from behind my ear. Once a voyeur I became a voyeur of all. I hide myself and watch. The crick in the Venetian blinds, the blaze of the white line between door and jamb. Behind these frames is where I feel most myself.}

Thousands of leaves fall. Amid those leaves is her image. This engrosses her so intently she ceases to pay attention to the blinds and the window through which she sees. She leans up against the blinds. She presses her body into the blinds so that they part, revealing to the outside world lines of her body. She trembles. She pushes hard against the blinds and in turn the window and the window finally gives: the glass does not shatter but pops free from the window frame, pops out onto the soft leaf-covered lawn. The glass does not break. The blinds cannot keep back the pressure she puts upon them and so she too falls into the yard. Tangled in the blinds she tumbles and crushes the glass beneath her. She pants and writhes, the strings of the blinds pull at her, tug and snap. Her body is hot with fascination at the self she sees against and amid the leaves. Her clothes are shredded in this violence; when she rises to her knees she is bare to the leaves —
— she plunges into her leaf-self.

[PLATE 52]

"Reading *Le Figaro*"

1878, 39³/₄ x 32

News is only fragments. For example: "She was killed some months ago by the falling of a tree in Virginia" and "I hope that you will speak right out in meeting with the world" and "When will this fearful slumber have an end?"

My mother is a pretty picture of pale yellow and cream white in bright afternoon sun. The chain that hangs from her black-framed glasses glitters. Her black hair shines. She sits with a newspaper open in her hands but she is asleep. The sun still keeps regular hours, but we are prey to sleep at any time. As are you. My mother sleeps in the chair by the big, brass mirror, which reads all the news upside down. My old mother's hand, bone and knuckle, skin taut and dry. Sleep is in all the news and there is something good to that: after all the catastrophes, self-inflicted, otherwise, it is only sleep that will undo us: we will sleep.

Our inability to stay awake makes travel too dangerous; I cannot see you and that breaks my heart.

A letter is like a newspaper and my letter is like the news. Written between sleep, about sleep.

I knew I wasn't immune to sleep the morning a vase of flowers withered *on the sudden*. Still morning, but not that morning or the next; I didn't know what morning.

Fires erased the suburbs, burned through factory-assembled colonials and particleboard ranch houses. Blaring smoke detectors and fire alarms were not loud enough to wake those asleep. After the electrical fires in the cities, charred and hollow buildings, mother and I began to keep most of our house unplugged. Our house: quiet and dark. We kept power only for the kitchen and the living room. You always loved our living room; you'd doze in the afternoon sun. We fall asleep on chairs and couches, on linoleum and carpets. We have food but I'm afraid we'll starve to death. I've been writing this letter for days.

Mother wakes. She reads about sleep, unsure for a moment what else to do. She stands and complains of terrible stiffness. We've stopped consulting the clock and the calendar, stopped trying to figure out *when* it is we are awake. Time is only too sad now. The fireplace is full of ashes, cold and damp. A mushroom sprouted in the ashes as if in an instant, and then a dozen more white fungi appeared.

If we dreamed while we slept I'd feel as if we were at least having that second life, but we don't and that's sad too. More than sad.

The living room is blue now.

Mother fell out of her chair — when, I don't know, nor how: did she rise to look out the window only to collapse, asleep again? I reach for my mother, wince at the sight of an open gash on her cheek, but before I can touch her old shoulder she is in her chair, crying, touching her face, and I'm on my back, on the floor. I say, "Mother?" Her cheekbone is broken. I wake, she's asleep. The gash beneath her eye is infected, alive, first aid won't be enough, but there is no other aid. We're all helpless beneath the blank gaze of sleep.

Mother sleeps more than I, now. I'm lonely, but I hope she won't wake up because she screams when she's awake.

My skirt is wet with my own urine. My skirt is stiff, dried, the cotton cracks like old cardboard. For days, I change into a fresh skirt. Like a beaver working to keep its teeth ground, I gnaw at my fingernails; I clip my toenails when I can; my hair teases the small of my back, falls into my eyes. Moments are connected only by my actions.

Here, in the country, the darkness outside is deep. I'm used to moving by the slight-light as the moon sets. Used to the numb trees and the spike darkness between. Animals come out of the forest and drop to the lawn, grass that has grown wild and high. Sleeping deer: these animals crash to the ground, their sleep-poses unnatural. There was a string of time during which I woke only in the small hours. After a while I could no longer imagine anything but hunger-ache and black grass and sleeping animals. A fox asleep next to my head. Broken-winged birds pepper every field. I hope some of the city remains and is brightly lit as cities are meant to be. I want us to be visible from space for as long as is humanly possible.

Mother is dead, her body by the fireplace. I am in the tall grass of the backyard. Newspapers have gathered around my body. A writing tablet finishes the hook of my hand. I'll never see you again, and who will send this letter? How many of us write during our brief periods of wakefulness? Is there any reason to document the world's great slumber?

[PLATE 53]

"Baby Reaching for an Apple"

1893, 39 ½ x 25 ¾

Young women labor for the fruits of knowledge; the modern woman must wrestle apples from men. Science is radiation poisoning. But that radiation! I have tried to make the general effect as bright, as gay, as amusing as possible, even as she holds a hank of her hair.

"Baby," says the baby's godmother, "My friend laments that you little ones have such small memories." The baby's godmother reaches into the tub, lifts a sopping and soapy sponge from the water and squeezes warm water over the baby's back. Baby splashes; godmother's blouse is quite wet; the window is open and summer sun and air swirls into the little bathroom. The baby's godmother speaks with a low voice, a sweet voice, and respectful — a voice for ghosts and fairies. "I told her that you remember. She said, 'She's only eight months.' 'I know how old she is,' I said. I said, 'What her godmother tells her, when her godmother visits, she remembers.' My friend didn't believe me at all, but, as you and I know, what matters is what's true, not what other people think is true."

The baby's godmother lifts the baby from tub to towel and gently dries the baby; the baby's hair is as light as dandelion seeds. The baby's godmother carries the baby downstairs, to the living room, to the back patio: the baby will remember how the sun and the breeze feel on her skin, all over her skin. The baby is soothed and dazzled.

"Let me show you the apple." The baby's godmother carries the child out into the yard. Grass dips in and out of the godmother's open-toed slippers. The way the grass moves, a great hand must be just above, fingers raking circles, grass like the groomed gravel in a Japanese garden but moving. The sky is gold and the sky is green.

Halfway across the yard is a line of apple trees. The baby's godmother brings the baby under one of the trees, seats the baby on her arm. "Do you see that apple?" godmother says. The baby looks up, reaches up. "That's right. That's the one. I have to tell you about that apple, the apple your great-grandmother wrote.

"Take a bloom of paper, Baby, flat squares of paper cut and built into fruit, pears, cherries, an apple." Sparrows fly quick in the air, from the trees to the house and back, fly into the branches and into the eaves where they nest. The apples are more yellow than red, green-yellow, round. The leaves on the tree are so full of green, they've stained the branches green. Godmother's dress is pink and like an orchard too. "The tree grew from a seed, a single seed, but this apple grew from a bud of paper your grandmother tied to this branch. Here she tied a crumpled ball of paper with her description of an apple written on the inside. Your grandmother's description was perfect. Try to think of words to describe the world, Baby; the world is only words rightly arranged."

The baby's godmother takes the branch from which the written apple hangs and gently pulls it toward the baby. The baby touches the apple; the baby will remember the way the skin of the apple felt, like wax paper wrapped around chilled cookie dough. The baby's godmother says, "My role is to teach you what you can't forget." She loves the weight of the baby on her arm, the feel of the baby's skin; whole and plump and growing. "Watch this apple, Baby. Watch as it grows on this same branch every year.

"Baby, one day when you're driving home, white blossoms will fall against your windshield and for an instant you'll be sure you're in a snowstorm. You'll be glad, because you love the snow, you were born during a November snow.

"You'll know the blossoms aren't snow — maybe not right away, but so quick it'll be as if you never thought otherwise. When the blossoms are in the air, your great-grandmother's written apple will begin to grow again.

"Now Baby, no one in your family has dared to pick this apple. We know we could never write another so well, we know our apple would taste bitter. But you, Baby, you'll come back home, you'll come to this tree and you won't hesitate."

[PLATE 54]

"Little Girl in a Blue Armchair"

1878, 35¼ x 51⅛

Degas corresponds blue to my little girl, a little girl who sits like an accident, and that's naturalism. Thank you, my dear M. Degas. Your brush, in the background, its tip the picture on a porcelain vase.

I remember Emily as the sort of child who used what came to her without question and with ease. A scarf, that afternoon. A scarf materialized on the floor of a closet, a forgotten cloth once belonging to Emily's mother. Emily wore it tied around her waist.

Emily sat on a chubby blue armchair. Against the blue of the chair, her white Communion dress was a spark. She held a white grease pencil in her hand, held the pencil above her head; I watched as she traced an outline of her body onto the chair-back. Before I could find the mental wherewithal to tell her to stop, stop ruining the upholstery, a dog barked. Emily slipped the grease pencil beneath her thigh, out of sight. Emily did not own a dog. Nor did her mother.

"Hello, Katherine," Emily said.

I couldn't locate the source of the bark; the furniture in that room, the sunny day room, was placed but not arranged, and so made many hidden spaces. Behind Emily, against the far wall, was a blue couch, beside it a blue chair, and to my left another blue chair. The dog barked again and I saw him, a little terrier, ensconced on the chair to my left.

"Whose dog is that?" Emily's mother was no figure of authority, so I tried to be, but Emily usually charmed me away from any stern or overly-adult behavior. I loved her deeply, stupidly, and drove to her mother's house once a week to spend time with her — not with her mother.

"He belongs to a little boy who lives down the lane."

I knew very well that there was no boy. I approached the dog, let him sniff at my hand, patted him and pushed him aside so I could sit down. The dog clambered up the soft arm of the chair and, once I'd settled in, found a spot on my lap. The dog wore a collar with a name tag: Edward.

"Edward," I said. The dog shrugged his eyebrows.

"Mom bought it for me," Emily said. This too, untrue.

"Did you name it?" I asked.

"Yes."

"A noble name for a dog. Get the pencil out from under your leg."

Emily produced the pencil.

"Have you ruined the furniture?" I asked.

"No. Look." She bounced off the chair and stepped aside. Left behind was a misshapen silhouette of Emily.

"That won't come off, you know," I said.

"It isn't supposed to."

I put Edward on the floor and contemplated what to do about Emily's graffiti. I turned the chair so it faced away from the door. "Your mother hardly ever comes in here," I said.

Emily said, "She never comes in here. This room is haunted and she's terrified of ghosts."

Emily's mother was out shopping. When I arrived that afternoon, she fixed us gin and tonics. When she was through with hers, she left. She and I had been roommates in college and our relationship remained remarkably the same. That is, she took advantage of me then, too. I let her. I still let her. That she takes advantage doesn't matter now because I get to spend time with Emily.

Emily said, "We should play astronauts."

"Where shall we go?" I asked.

Emily pointed to the blue couch. "Pluto," she said. She added, "I don't think Pluto's a real planet."

When I asked her why she thought Pluto wasn't a real planet she told me that Pluto was solid ice and too small to be a planet. She explained, very thoroughly, why she was convinced there was life on Pluto. Had I been at a party, and had a man claiming to be a scientist told me what Emily told me, I would have believed him. Emily's age and her inclination to invent was all that gave me cause to doubt her theory, and even still. Edward barked. We played astronauts for a long time. Finally, the umbilical attached to Emily's space suit—the plaid scarf—unraveled, and she floated off into space. I explained how I could rescue her, but she said no, and that my plan was impractical. She said, "Save yourself." She floated out of the day room, through a rectangle of sunlight, into the dark hallway. For a while—just long enough for me to wonder what was going on—Edward and I sat in the day room alone, waiting for Emily to return.

When she did the three of us fell asleep on the couch. When I woke, I saw Emily's mother standing at the doorway of the room. I said, "We must have fallen asleep." By the time I'd completed my sentence, Emily's mother was gone.

Edward followed when I carried Emily to her room. Just as I was about to leave, Emily said, "I found Edward in the woods."

A little less than a month later I went to visit Emily but found the house empty. Not everything was gone, but Emily and her mother, certainly, permanently. I called out their names. I walked around the house, through the partially empty rooms until I came to the day room, where all the blue furniture had been left.

I pushed Emily's chair, the chair marked with her white silhouette, across the polished hardwood floors; it ground a trail into the polish. At the front door, where I struggled to angle the chair in such a way as to allow its release, I realized the chair wouldn't fit in my car. Nor, really, in my apartment. I lived in such a small apartment. I sat on the chair and stared out the front door, across the white stone drive, past my car and into the woods. The sun was lowering itself to the trees, black trees, leafless. On the other side of the sky, past a thick cloud of man-made satellites, were the planets, untrammeled planets, dust and ice planets.

Emily's mother had hitched herself to a new husband, I supposed, and when that unraveled or just got numb I'd receive another letter urging me to come for a visit.

[PLATE 55]

"Young Woman in Black"

1883, 31½ x 25¼

A somber interest in family: I didn't take "Young Woman in Black" back to Philadelphia, but she remained in my hands until late in my life. That is, the bitter end.

Sister sits at the window. Rain falls, a hot summer rain, fat drops loud against the glass. With her hearing aid out, she barely hears the rain at all. She can barely see it, either. Brother is dead. His funeral is today.

In her home, Sister's family cleans the dishes from brunch. Sister made a mess of her poached eggs, hates the way she has to eat, feeling around the dish with her swollen fingers, guiding her fork.

Her niece asks if she needs more light. "No," says Sister. She is old, so her needs are often asked after, even those which she could easily attend to, as if she might not even know what her needs are.

Through her black veil, there is the plum of Sister's mouth.

She closes her eyes.

Will the rain keep up?

Sleep comes and goes for Sister, in bed or out, and so her dreams—always as vivid as life—are difficult to distinguish from life. Some are as mundane. She dreams that she is in the room she is in now, and that she is seated by the window as she is. The clouds break, and all is green and gold and dripping. Her sight is as good as it ever was. A brown rabbit zigzags across the grass. A cardinal as bright as a holly berry—oh, there is a holly bush in the yard, like the one at the end of the driveway of the house where Brother and I grew up—how had she not noticed? And where is Brother? Surely he would like to see.

She opens the window—it swings out, on a hinge like a door—I don't remember this window working like that—and she steps out onto bark mulch, then steps onto the lawn. She crosses the yard—the cardinal remains still as she approaches—she is able to touch the bird, hold the bird, she feels its heart beat beneath its soft breast. The bird's feathers are dry, even though drops of water hang from every leaf.

She releases the bird. Green, red, blue.

Sister pushes through trees. Her clothes become soaked, but as soon as she steps into the sun, they dry. Where the road was, is a river. At the edge of the river is a wooden tub. She climbs into it and pushes it free from the shore.

The tub bobs as it floats to the center of the river and catches the current. She lies on her back. Branches reach over the river, the sun lights the leaves. Some branches hang so low, the leaves stroke her face. Even in her old body, she feels young. She is young.

Sister's niece gently wakes her and says it's time to go.

The rain has stopped. Sunlight on the yard. Sister puts her hand to the window. Oh yes right this one doesn't open. Her legs are very stiff and she needs her niece to help her to her feet.

Time for Brother's funeral.

"Study for At the Opera"
1878, 5 x 8 ¹/₂;

"Study for At the Opera"
1878, 4 x 6;

"At the Opera"
1878, 32 x 26

I picked up a preference for pocket-sized sketchbooks from Degas. In this way, I made notes for my paintings, and could work in the most unexpected locations. Here, refine an idea into a finished composition.

A woman watched an opera about torture. She long ago lost the thread of the opera's narrative, her mind lost in the woven fabric of a black cloth sack. She sat alone in a mezzanine box. The view wasn't ideal for seeing the opera, but at times the music shifted and filled the box, as if the performers were seated up in a dark corner, up somewhere near the woman's left ear. The woman raised a pair of brass opera glasses to her eyes; by their magnification, she saw the grimace of the man forced to crouch naked on the stage. A wood pole and a triangle of rope kept his pose rigid. His face shone with sweat. His teeth. The woman unfolded her fan and stirred the air about her face.

She rested her opera glasses on her lap, in the basket of her dress — she was distracted by a subtle change in the light on the wall to her left. A black rectangle, the size of a door, grew light, a little light, just a shade. She could not locate the edges of the rectangle, not exactly. When her eyes focused on any one segment of the rectangle's black border, the border vibrated, became less of a border. How irritating this was to her mind. To her right, in a box like her own, sat a man and a woman, deeply engaged in the actions of the stage; the stage.

A chorus of blindfolded men. A man, tied to a plank, was lowered headfirst into a bucket of dirty water. This water-boarded man sang gasps: choke and spit. A boy, held down with electrical tape, taped so tight he couldn't avoid the blast of air blown up his nostrils, sang high-pitched bursts. Their songs were swallowed by the chorus. A soldier kept time with his boots. The stage was littered with rope, this was set. The set. The curtains were rust-red razor wire.

In the box to the right: the man scans the audience with his opera glasses; the woman sews.

The rectangle on the wall was silver, now, silver like photo-silver, a silver gelatin print. Indeed, the silver developed, she thought, and as if her thought was transferred to the rectangle, an image began to develop. When she watched the rectangle on the wall to her left, she was not watching the opera *per se;* the performance went on, endlessly. The woman fanned herself again. Raised her opera glasses again. A bare light bulb, a shining pear at the end of a black vine, dangled over a weeping boy. The bulb swung, pendulum-like, and crept closer and closer to the top of the weeping boy's head. Eventually, the bulb would hit the weeping boy. The question on the minds of all in the audience: Would the bulb shatter? And if it did, would the audience be left blind in the dark and damp air? The image on the rectangle took shape. A man seated and blanketed by shadow. Not a man, a woman in a black dress.

The woman studied the rectangle with her opera glasses. The opera's libretto was covered with agitation. With non-words. The songs bordered cacophony. Voices in cement rooms and corridors, muffled voices, conversations barely overheard, monologues delivered in other languages. Food, masticated. What songs? Regurgitated. The image on the rectangle was her own image. As she had stared at the rectangle, the image of herself stared back. The man in the box to her right stared at her too. Through opera glasses, he watched her, to see if she would betray herself. The woman seated beside the man, the sewing woman, sweated as she stitched. On the stage below, members of the chorus piled on top of each other. Their robes opened; beneath their robes they were naked. They clambered over one another, a swarm. The man forced to crouch bit hard on a piece of hairy rope. His eyes squeezed shut.

A wind filled the opera house. This was a breath from an enormous head.

The man in the box to her right watched and he opened his mouth wide. He bared his teeth. He wet his teeth with his tongue. The sewing woman sewed quickly, pricking herself often. Finally, the sewing woman put down her needle. She pointed to the woman who still stared at the rectangle, who was mesmerized by her own likeness. The sewing woman had made a hood, using fabric from her own clothes.

The woman asked — of course — "Why am I here?" and said —

The bulb shattered against the weeping boy's head —

"Please let me die."

And yes, the audience, left in the dark and damp air.

[PLATE 59]

"Lady at the Tea Table"
1883, 29 x 24

Mrs. Riddle and her daughter didn't like this portrait. Mrs. Riddle's cousinage of gifts, stacking tea sets, the smallest of which bore cup handles too tiny for even a baby's hand and are lost inside cups much larger. If I am not careful, I might choke on a sugar bowl.

My daughter had never met her great aunt and I hadn't seen my aunt in ten years. I expected her to be unchanged: stern in appearance and first impression, yet generous with house, story, and food. And kind, but never sentimental. Ten years ago, she was seventy, but her brow was smooth and she moved with vigor.

My expectation was naïve. My daughter was frightened by my aunt's appearance and no wonder — she was unwell, a froth of saliva collected at the corners of her mouth, she was too thin, and she trembled. From a dim corner of the room emerged a woman my own age, a cousin I hardly knew and who made little impression other than that she was short and powered by irritation.

"Your aunt is very pleased to see you," my cousin said. Without turning to look at my daughter she added, "And pleased at last to meet you. She wonders why she hasn't met you sooner."

This was a slight directed at me. I ignored my cousin and introduced my aunt to her great-niece. My daughter attempted a little curtsy, a gesture she'd practiced with great gusto on the train, much to the amusement of our fellow passengers. In the wilting presence of my aunt and cousin, though, my daughter only slid a little lower on my leg while bowing her head. My aunt smiled, and I recognized her then as the woman I'd known.

Set in front of my aunt on the table was a porcelain tea set, Dutch scenes set in cobalt. I walked along the left edge of the table, my daughter close behind, and sat by my aunt. "Auntie," I said, "it's so good to see you." My aunt stared, past the porcelain and me and my daughter, at the bare wall on the other side of the room. She said, "You know this tea set was buried upstate for seventeen years. Buried along with the ebony chair and three family paintings, valuable paintings, one of a red cottage just poking out from behind a grassy hillock; one depicting an Amish house-cutting; and, finally, the most valuable, a little painting of a girl in a white dress, as pretty as you are, sweet pea." My aunt gave a soft look to my daughter. "As pretty, and wearing a dress like yours, except for the silver, there was silver needlework on the bodice, really another portrait of another little girl. What a painting.

"As you know, we had all this buried, to protect it from my mother's ex-husband, who claimed all these nice things were his, and sent lawyers and detectives after them, but never found them. They were buried for seventeen years, and even mother forgot about them, but she left a map, you know." My aunt gave me a look I found hard to interpret, but guessed she expected me to confirm that there was a map, that I'd seen it, which I hadn't, so I only nodded, ambiguously. Where my cousin stood, behind my aunt, the light made her look almost pretty, dimming certain of her features, while lighting up her hair and drawing a line along her slender neck. The tea set, I knew, was a gift from my mother, and had never been buried in upstate New York.

I leaned close to tell my aunt that we weren't staying, we were just dropping by, so she could meet her niece, so we could say hello. My aunt wasn't well. I didn't wish to impose. But before I said a word my aunt spoke again:

"This morning, before you two ladies came by — come a little closer, dear," she urged my daughter, " — this morning a little circle of light appeared on my bedroom wall. My room was already bright from the morning sun, but this circle was brighter. Inside that circle of light glass birds flew and glass squirrels jumped. It was a circus concert, and those animals, they were glass but alive. I knew the animals were there, dancing in that spotlight for a reason, to tell me something, about a man at first, I thought, the man standing in my doorway. He was so handsome. You know I think I knew him." My aunt turned her attention to my daughter. "In truth, sweetheart, the animals were telling me that you were coming today, and that I needed to get dressed and out of bed, and that you would want to see the tea set my mother had buried for so long." My aunt held up a cup, and I was again impressed by the rich color, impressed as I had been when I first saw the set, in a shop with my mother, when I was a little girl.

My aunt said, to my daughter, "Do you know how to speak by only dancing?"

I expected my daughter to shake her head, to say no she didn't, but instead my daughter said yes, and produced for my aunt a deep, flourishing curtsy, more elegant than those she'd rehearsed on the train. Grand and colorful. Her curtsy earned her happy laughter from my aunt.

Shortly before we left I excused myself, as my daughter chatted away and my aunt listened patiently. The toilet was as I remembered it from my childhood visit, a pull-chain toilet with a high, wooden tank, the little room dark and heavy with the smell of potpourri. Next to the mirror, above the sink, was a framed piece of paper I didn't recall. The paper was lined notebook paper. A soft crease ran from top to bottom. Drawn with black ink was a simple line surrounded by landmarks, each captioned: "the oak," "the stone wall," "the well," etc. Along the bottom of the page was a list, slightly obscured by the frame, and it was this list that caused me to doubt my memory of how things were. The list read, "three paintings; ebony chair; tea service."

My aged aunt, her memories more real than my own.

[PLATE 60]

"Five O'Clock Tea"

1880, 25¹/₂ x36¹/₂

If it were me, I would ask, "Where is the rest of this canvas? Is this anticipation, or is this mystery?" The girls wear their hats and gloves. Read: what could that mean? Wherever there is pressure from a pencil, the soft ground adheres and exposes, and so when immersed, lines are bitten in.

At her daughter's request, behest, a little begging, Mom put out the silver tea set. She worried over it a little, cleaned up the tarnish, considered how sad she'd be if the teapot was dented, this heirloom set, a prize passed from mother to mother—but Mom recalled her own girlhood desire to play five o'clock tea with the silver tea set and how good it would be for the set to be used by someone, anyone, better it be used by her daughter and her daughter's ten-year-old friends. Only three girls had been invited. Easy enough to keep track of.

Mom looked at her watch, up at the yellow kitchen clock. The girls were due to arrive shortly for her daughter's birthday tea party. They all decided to dress up—her daughter was in her room, bouncing up and down, to watch the ruffle of her once-Easter dress rise and settle. Four girls for a fancy tea party and then mischief, no doubt, ruined dresses and fun for a few hours. Mom looked at her watch, then the kitchen clock. Her son was due home from a sleepover soon. He was a good older brother, he would stay out of the girls' way, and anyhow, his sister still found him wonderful, at least most of the time. Maybe he'd have a slice of cake and sit for some tea.

The phone rang, it was the mother of one of the girls, a little girl too sick to come, sorry, they waited until the last minute to see, but she's too sick to go out and probably won't be in school on Monday. Soon after, a second call, another girl couldn't come, a family emergency, the whole family driving up to New Paltz to see Grandma, very possibly for the last time. Mom said, "I'm so sorry, I hope things turn for the good, my thoughts are with you." In truth, Mom's thoughts were focused on her daughter, soon to be disappointed. At least one girl was still coming.

Elementary school friends establish hierarchies; unfortunately the birthday girl's number one friend and number two friend were the girls unable to attend the tea party. Mom knew, in a vague way, about this order—there was little subtlety involved. So Mom had a sense that the girl coming—the doorbell rang—would be, on her own, a letdown.

As the birthday girl came dashing to the top of the stairs, Mom apprised her of the situation, then, before the birthday girl could react, Mom opened the front door. There stood the least friend, dumped off by her mother. The least friend was dressed in a navy blue dress, wore a hat, yellow gloves, and held a box wrapped in gold paper. She looked very beautiful, Mom thought.

The least friend said, "Happy Birthday," and curtsied, a gesture worked out in the least friend's bedroom that morning. Mom was amused and Mom was pleased that her daughter did not betray any disappointment, but curtsied back and took the box and led the least friend into the living room, where the silver tea set was on the table, along with the white and blue teacups. The two girls sat side-by-side on the flower couch (as the birthday girl called it) and Mom—as their server—explained the tea and the little snacks to come, a lunch of junk food, capped with cake. On the mantel, Mom explained, were party favors for four, but since the other girls couldn't come, "You can each have two."

This was the first the least friend had heard that the other girls wouldn't be coming—and she could not help but smile. Here was her chance to improve her status with the birthday girl.

Improve her status she did not: "Open your present!" she said and the birthday girl did (what a beautiful, adult wrapping job). The gift was a model kit, an airplane. The birthday girl thought—"Why did she get a gift for a boy?" Mom thought—"Oh, my little girl, this is so disappointing." The least friend only smiled, pleased with herself.

The model's package depicted an airplane flying through the sky. The plane looked like a Christmas ornament, all shiny-glass colors: red, green, and silver. From the canopied cockpit a little man waved and smiled. The wings were clear, like the wings of the pedal-powered glider at the science museum. The package declared, "Golden sugar-powered engine enclosed!! No batteries needed!!" And again, in French.

Mom said, "Well isn't that wonderful."

The birthday girl, still valiantly hiding her disappointment (though thinking "Brother better have bought me something nice.") said, "Thanks."

Before the least friend could speak—she was about to say, "Open it up!" Mom said, "I should get the pizza nuggets out of the oven."

The birthday girl sat holding the box while her mother went into the kitchen. The least friend, unable to bear waiting, said, "Open the package!" The birthday girl looked at the box again and said, "What's a sugar-powered engine?" Mom carried in a plate of hot snacks and said, "Just a minute and I'll have some chips." Then she looked at the least friend and said to the birthday girl, "Open it. You should put it together." Mom didn't leave to get the chips

—and Brother came in.

Twelve years old, awkward and always nervous, Brother mustered the calm to say, "Happy Birthday I'll go upstairs to my room."

The birthday girl said, "No!"

And Mom said, "Stay."

Brother waved awkwardly at the least friend and sat down across from the girls.

The least friend said, "You were opening the model." The birthday girl unfolded the cardboard box. The model appeared to be nothing too complex. A fuselage, two wings, a little man to seat in the cockpit. "All the parts are so shiny," Mom said. She found she was taken by the toy, even as it was, in pieces.

"We don't need paints," the least friend said. She picked up a wing and the fuselage. "Or glue."

The birthday girl tilted the box and out slid a little plastic packet — inside the packet, a slip of paper and the golden engine. Brother told Sister to open the packet, and she did. He reached for the slip of paper; the birthday girl lifted the engine up and let it shine in the light. The least friend watched, so pleased she wanted to shout, or slap someone. She ate a mozzarella stick, crammed the whole thing in her mouth, even though it burned her palate tender.

Brother said, "It's not sugar. The engine runs on baking soda. And vinegar." Brother pointed to the engine — "There and there" — he said, pointing out the little openings where the baking soda and then the vinegar would go. "Let's put this together and see what it can do."

The birthday girl said, "I want to," and began to pop the pieces in place. "Where does the engine go?" she asked. The least friend touched the side of the fuselage and slid up a little door — the inside of the plane visible for a moment before the birthday girl placed the engine — little rods and gears; a gear on the engine now enmeshed with a gear inside the plane.

The least friend handed the birthday girl the landing gear, the last piece to be attached. In slid the pilot, and Mom went out to the kitchen for the fuel required. From the kitchen she said, "I think we have vinegar and if we don't I can run out to the store." And then, "Here we go!" Mom rushed, excited to see what the plane would do. The propeller would spin, she guessed, but she hoped for more.

Plates were moved aside to make a runway of the coffee table; the airplane was set down; the door in the fuselage was opened and baking soda was measured into the engine; the door was closed; the airplane sat on the runway, glittering silver like the teapot that stood at the end of the runway. A little vinegar was poured—by Mom—into an opening at the top of the fuselage. A fizz, a plastic grind and then a smooth whine; the propeller spun and the wheels beneath the plane, too. The wheels spun out on the polish of the coffee table, then gripped the table, and the plane took off.

At first its flight was feeble. A crash in the fireplace looked to be the plane's inevitable end, but instead the plane steadied, picked up speed and looped over—upside down, then, again, right side up—and flew back at the coffee table. A perfectly piloted flight. Except for the crash into the silver teapot.

Not a dreadful crash. The airplane swerved down the runway, bounced up over the lip of the tray on which the teapot sat, and nosed into the teapot— Mom's heart leapt a little—but without enough force to damage the airplane or the pot.

The birthday girl—some time during the model plane's flight—had reached out and taken her friend's hand; the two girls' mouths were wide open with wonder.

[PLATE 61]

"Lydia Leaning on Her Arms, Seated in a Loge"
1879, 21⅝ x 17¾

The light that lights the canvas is Lydia. "If the reflected girl is also the girl at the center of the picture, Manet shifted his position as spectator." Here, the mirror is not behind the subject, but is the subject. Lydia does not face us, as she appears to; she faces the mirror, and so, Lydia is not in the painting at all.

[Prelude]

Lydia's little boy looks at Lydia, her yellow-green dress, and in her dress he sees the hills where he and Lydia have been, where he has been in her arms, the foothills not a mile from their apartment. The little boy puts his hand on Lydia's dress, she touches his head, he touches her thighs and the cloth stretched between. Lydia's dress is silk, smooth like the stone the little boy recently found on a walk with Lydia.

Lydia remembers the hills, she walks them when the weather permits, near the river, with her son. Her memory is not the little boy's memory. The boy's memories are lost, he is only one year old. And what fascinates the little boy often goes unnoticed by Lydia. The boy stands, pulling at Lydia's dress for support. Lydia touches her son's shoulders, she smiles, she is entertaining a visitor called Gray.

[Gray Visits]

A long time has passed since Lydia has entertained a guest. She used to entertain a lot, even when she was pregnant, her apartment filled with her friends, young men and women, many still single, still hoping to attend the right party, where they would meet someone who could make them happy. Lydia's former work friend is Gray; Gray is the name she uses in the office where Lydia once worked. Gray hasn't been by in a year, though the two women have kept sporadically in touch.

Gray tucks a ring of hair behind her ear and watches herself in the mirror; the mirror stands behind Lydia. Lydia sees that Gray's eyes follow Gray's own reflection, and are not on Lydia. Lydia has felt that way since she announced she was pregnant, that is, Lydia has felt unwatched—except by her son, whose attentions are intense. Lydia casts her own eyes down, to her lap, where her son was a moment ago (now he is on the floor, crawling between Lydia and Gray's chairs). The skirt of Lydia's dress is like the scorched foothills where she takes her baby for long walks. Lydia's arms are stronger than they've ever been. She leans forward, onto her arms, examines the fingers of one hand with the other and then vice versa. Behind Lydia, the mirror sparkles, and within there is a second ceiling light and a second band of sunlight, slanting into the apartment—afternoon winter light. The baby crawls golden into this light. Lydia tells Gray about a morning a few mornings ago.

[Lydia's Conversation with Gray]

"The bridge shone with rain as we crossed to the bakery for our breakfast roll. Clouds moved low in the sky but there were breaks in the clouds, and so white light moved across the big mountain in the heart of town. The light was like the blank page between chapters.

"I saw a man in a rust-colored suit waiting at the intersection. I thought he was waiting to cross the street but when the crossing signal changed he stayed where he was. I felt drops of rain then, hot, soft drops, and the air was stifling, crowded with a dusty smell. I covered the baby's head with my hand, because when the drops hit him, I saw him wince.

"The glass of the display case at the bakery dripped condensation. My roll was warm and as I ate the steam from it warmed and moistened the tip of my nose. Baby slept, warm against my chest.

"As I walked home, in the rain, my shawl over the baby's head, I saw, again, the man in the rust-colored suit and I thought of an expression my grandmother used. She would say, when I visited and there was rain, 'You brought the rain with you.' This was a fond, sweet thing to say, as if the world only existed where I was, as if the world revolved around me. And now I understand perfectly that it did. Now my world revolves around him." Lydia looks at the baby, who is looking up, at nothing, or into the beam of light, or perhaps at the reflections behind Lydia. "But when I thought of it I didn't feel kind or warm or good. The man in the rust-colored suit was responsible for the rain, he brought it like a shroud, and I became certain he had come to town to steal my baby, and really, Gray, my fear of this is so real, well, I haven't gone out since that morning, I've been mad with worry, and that's why I finally asked you to come over, I know it's inconvenient."

"Nonsense," Gray says, and, "Nonsense about the man wanting your son. You know this is a safe town and no one means you or your son any harm. Look at him, what a beautiful child. I'm only sorry I haven't been by before, he's such a pleasure to be around, he hasn't made a peep. Your man who brought the rain was just a man—ill-dressed for the weather, it sounds—not some reaper to take your baby back over the wall."

[Epilogue]

The wall between the living and the ether that surrounds the living, Gray meant. What is everyday, what is commonplace, is not. The little boy approaches an electric outlet, uncapped, open, out-of-use, and there is light there, as the boy remembers light, endless and indestructible. The child's desire to touch the outlet is strong; it is like the desire to touch his mother's face.

Lydia snatches her son up from the floor, "Oh, you little explorer," she says, upset and glad. Deeply in love, Lydia wants her son in this world, and she makes light too, with songs, her face, with the taste of her nipples and the milk that she makes and gives to the boy.

[PLATE 62]

"The Cup of Tea"
1880, 36¼ x 25¾

Like music, pollen is carried by air, by birds, and on the legs of bees. Even across great bodies of water. A single flower, like a daub of paint, can be found growing in a peck of dirt on a rock in the middle of the ocean. As I painted, I saw the flower behind my subject's head blossom into a thought.

When I was a little girl I had a friend named Adam who would do anything I asked. During the last summer we had together — we were eight? — he was reliably at my door every morning, just as soon as his mother would let him out, slathered in sunblock and dressed in square blue shorts, a t-shirt either green, red or white, and Velcro sneakers. He was a beautiful boy, my mother always said. If I was still eating when he arrived, he sat at the table with me and often I'd tell him to finish my bowl of cereal and he was always thrilled to, because my mother bought cereal he was strictly forbidden to have, chocolate chip cereal and frosted cereal with dehydrated marshmallows. He even drank the milk.

My house — actually across town from his, quite a bike ride — was right on the bay. A stretch of sea grass and a narrow beach was all that kept the house from the sea and often enough, when there was a big storm, the ocean was beneath our deck, right up against the house. During stormy nights I was afraid sharks would swim inside. One time I told Adam that a shark had swum into my living room and that by leaning over the edge of the dining room table I had been able to touch its fin. He was terrified and thrilled.

We waded through the tall sea grass in anticipation of the sea. All the grass leaned toward my house except the grass where Adam and I made our trails; we bent the grass outward, toward the boats in the bay. The bell of a buoy rang when the breeze would perk up and Adam would stop to listen and say, "It's three o'clock." I didn't get this until later, when I was taken to church by a friend and heard the bells chime the hour; I thought of Adam then and wondered where he was. Among the sea grass were holes, bored into the mud by crabs that we tried to goad with stalks of plucked grass. I told Adam that the roots of the grass were edible and he ate some.

Sand didn't hold our interest the way the grass did and so once we arrived on the beach we ran for the rock jetty. Where the jetty met the beach was a tide pool, which we played around for hours: on the other side of the jetty was a rowboat, tied to a wooden post. "Adam," I said. "A boat." At the bottom of the boat was a pool of dirty water. Adam said, "It's sinking." I said, "No, stupid, water just got in over the sides. We have to bail. Haven't you ever heard of bailing?" I knew nothing about boats, except that I'd been on them, but my desire, the desire to captain my own boat, made me certain. "Let's row across the bay," I said. Adam said, "But we haven't got oars." I told him that we could use our hands and I pointed — from where we stood, the other side of the bay was visible through a copse of anchored yachts — "It's not that far."

We climbed down the jetty into the boat. I began to bail the water out with cupped hands and told Adam to do the same. Once I grew impatient with bailing I told Adam to untie the rope. He leaned out — dangerously tilting the boat — and grabbed the rope. "It's a loop," he said and he said, "Try to bring the boat over this way." I tried to paddle the water, but tilted up as I was I could hardly reach. Frustrated, I yelled, "Pull the rope." He did and I nearly fell over. Adam grabbed the wooden post — hugged it — and then lifted the loop.

The boat drifted. First it bumped gently against the wooden post it had been tied to, but then began to move out into the bay. I was thrilled, but I could see that Adam was worried. "What?" I asked. "We're floating out to sea," he said. I said, "This isn't really the sea, Adam, this is a bay. It's like a tide pool. And we want to be floating out. And if we start to paddle — lean over your side and paddle." With our hands we paddled. The water was green near the jetty, and I could see the sand beneath. I didn't think about paddling but paddled and watched my own shadow, and the boat's shadow, move across the sand beneath the water. Adam said, "It's really very shallow." I didn't say anything, and almost without my noticing my shadow vanished, as did the sea floor. I looked up — I figured we were half-way there — but we weren't, a couple dozen feet from the jetty at most. "This is hard work," Adam said, and I paddled a little more furiously. "We have to paddle the same," I said, "or we'll just go in circles." Light shone up into my face from the water, which was deep green, like the tips of the sea grass behind my house. Adam said, "This is taking forever."

The clang of the buoy made us both jump; we were closer to the bell than ever before.

Our boat gently banged against the side of a yacht. We both sat still, afraid someone would lean over and yell at us. After a moment passed, I said, "No one's on board." So we used the side of the yacht, pushing ourselves along with our hands, pushing off from the bow of the yacht — the yacht, white, giant.

"What if a fish knocks us over?" Adam asked.

I told him that fish wouldn't bother us and, "Besides," I said, "the fish in a bay are all small fish."

"I thought you said there were sharks."

"Only when there's a storm."

What I thought would be a quick trip took hours. Adam said, "Your mom's going call us for lunch soon and then we're going to be in trouble."

"Just paddle," I said. He did but he was worried and I knew he was right.

When I looked back for the jetty, I found that I couldn't see it any more; my view was blocked by yachts, head-shaking yachts with little flapping flags. I wanted to dive into the water and when, miraculously it seemed, I could see the sand below our boat, I did.

Adam shouted and thrashed around in our boat in a panic until I popped my head up on his side of the boat and told him I was fine and, "Look, we're nearly there." We were still a good distance from the shore, and with neither of us paddling, the boat began to drift back out into the bay. Adam pulled me onto the boat. Soaked, I was cold in the breeze; the sun dried my clothes quickly, dried them stiff with salt. We made it to the shore. We dragged our little rowboat onto the beach and for a while we just lay on the sand, panting, eyes shut to the bright sun, holding hands.

The reason I'm telling you this story isn't because of the boat misadventure Adam and I had that last summer he and I were together. I'm telling you this story because of what we saw on the other side of the bay, and what we saw was this:

A woman in a peach-colored dress, sitting on her front lawn, drinking a cup of tea. She wore a hat that matched her dress. She had her chair in front of a house, her house, I presumed. Just to the right of her head was a window box with flowers in full bloom. Adam and I were going to ask the woman if she would let us call my mother, to lie to her about where we were. We walked—hand-in-hand, I remember—unselfconsciously—we walked hand-in-hand toward the woman until the door to her house opened. We froze when the front door to the woman's cute little seaside house opened and an enormous white horse stepped out onto the front walk. A massive horse, the kind that would pull a wagon in a team, and brilliantly white, all the more so for the bright sun and the glittering sand. The horse—unlike the woman who still sat drinking her tea—sensed us; it sniffed the air and turned its head. And when it did, Adam and I both saw that the horse had two heads. We saw that the horse wasn't just a horse, and just as certainly, we were not just on the other side of the bay, but someplace elsewhere.

[PLATE 63]

"Susan on a Balcony Holding a Dog"

1882, 39 ½ x 25 ½

Here, I make a final reference to my interest in light: sometimes, I've gone into a room, under the impression that a lamp was left on, only to see that the light was not lamp-light, but that a brilliant patch of sun got in.

Susan thought of her legs as dead. Bitten by spiders, left ankle, right calf, bitten when she was twelve, her legs did not grow with her body. Her legs were hidden beneath her dress. So many said, "Sad, Susan's face is so beautiful, a shame her wasted legs." Susan thought less and less about her legs. She thought more often about her city.

Carried out by the maid, ostensibly "for air," but truthfully to be out of the way, Susan sat in a wicker chair on the balcony of her father's Paris apartment. The Yorkshire terrier, Moss, found a staircase to Susan's lap—planter, wicker side table. Once on her tiny lap, Moss settled in to watch birds, little birds that made light branches bob; Moss looked down at the tops of trees, watched for movement. Susan rested a gloved hand on Moss's back, her other hand on her lap, beneath Moss. Susan was hot, overdressed. Her maids dressed her as if shriveled legs made one susceptible to drafts. The maids, as they fussed with Susan's collar, said, "We wouldn't want you to catch a cold."

Indeed. Susan stewed in her white dress and hat. She didn't entirely mind, though; the heat became something soothing, and Susan's mind was off elsewhere.

Her mind was on the long-empty Garden of Eden, located somewhere in Paris. This was not her own idea, that Eden was in Paris; this came from the pages of Charles Baudelaire's unwritten prose cycle which famously states, "Paris rots where Eden was." This idea was borrowed by Baudelaire from Aloysius Bertrand, who said: "Where now is Paris was The Garden. Decay began here." This is fiction and this is true. The city behind Susan is Paris and within Paris is the great courtyard Eden. There was the Garden, where Adam was made from mud and Eve from bone. So, Eden is a decrepit courtyard in Paris. So, behind Susan is Eden, Paris and the Seine, a filthy river alive with animals, familiar creatures and others, including the great river creature, mud-slick and half buried, endlessly suckling at river silt.

Susan's neck and stomach were damp with perspiration. She mopped her brow with a lace handkerchief. It looked pretty and was monogrammed but was not much for mopping brows. The British archaeologists in Cairo, who spent their days unentombing mummies, had piles of handkerchiefs for brow-mopping. In the desert, a sodden handkerchief dried almost instantly. The British archeologists knew how to enjoy heat. They sat under umbrellas and sipped gin and oversaw the labor of local men, descendants of the very slaves who built the tombs for the pharaohs, the tombs the British took apart for . . . why? Susan wondered. She answered her own question immediately; the keenness of her brain cooled her whole body: the British archaeologists wanted to know what happened after death, and Egyptian tombs are like gigantic tape recorders, memorizing the journey of the dead from this side of the river to the other.

Susan knew all about what happens to a person when they die. She'd known since she was a girl. When the spiders bit her, her parents called the priest. As he traveled from the church to her bed, she had a vision, a gift from the spiders and from God.

When a person dies, she knew, they travel to the afterlife through space, because the afterlife is on the other end of space, just on the outside of space. From Paris a person travels through the atmosphere into the solar system they grew up in, then onto the next solar system. There's infinite time, but there's infinite space, too, so there's no time to stop and explore every world, comet, star, etc., no matter how appealing. And all worlds and comets and stars are appealing. The universe is beautiful, nearly everyone realizes. Those who don't think so are in Hell. Some parts of the universe are so bright they look almost like the sky on a clear afternoon. This journey to the after-life can be quite disorienting; those who worry too much about up and down suffer but eventually they are saved. The trip is not lonely, because people die at the same time all the time; we fall in love with everybody who dies when we do.

Susan said to Moss, "God was wise to give the animals in Eden so much time to evolve." Susan knew about the creature in the Seine. She was calm about it. Prehistoric river creatures didn't worry her; nothing worried Susan. Except, maybe, that she might find herself bored. When the river creature finally bothered to lift a tentacle from the slurry and slime, when its poison-tipped finger touched Susan's shoulder—she was only too ready for death.

What is true is hard to establish. There is Eden and The End; there is Paris, crumbling onward with its beasts; there is a dog named Moss and there is the sun. There is also Susan, and her white dress buzzes with light. We know Susan was bitten by spiders, we know slaves built the pyramids, and we know that Baudelaire was a poet who read Bertrand.

[PLATE 64]

"Girl Arranging Her Hair"

1886, 29½ x 24½

I made a bet with Degas that I could take an ugly subject and make it fine. He said I'd only win if I made ugly beautiful. Once I began to paint, I felt as if I was cheating, because nothing is ugly once the eye sees the subject as color and color alone.

Holding a bottle of beer was still a thrill, and this thrill was magnified because I was outside, in the front of a gas station, with a group of guys — the band and a few other guys. I was seventeen. The bottle was brown and glass, the label sweat-rippled. A summer night, but cool. Very dark. Just a handful of miles from Ontario but still in the United States and feeling very American, aware of my American-ness — no doubt in part because of the local resentment toward Canadians. Reasonless. The gas station was yellow-lit, lit by the big roof over the pumps, lights cluttered with dead bugs, live bugs, webs, and leaves. Yellow-lit by the big plastic Sunoco sign. I stood away from the pumps, in a triangle of shadow.

I had new shoes and so was very aware of my feet, the little pebbles that ground between my heels and the crumbled cement. A few of the guys were inside, buying chips and cigarettes. The drummer and guitarist stood near where I stood, smoking and talking about the show, which was a good show, they had made a little cash and the guitarist met a girl, Kristine, who said she might catch us later if we wound up at the party in Martell, the next town over. I kind of listened to the drummer and the guitarist, but mostly looked around, worried a cop would show but also just looking. I felt good. I was included here, the guys liked me, they'd been looking out for me all week. I let the beer slip a little, caught it, brought it to my mouth—still cool. A hot day, till seven when the sun finally set, and slowly cool followed, blown in from across the border. I kicked a stone and an RV pulling a flatbed trailer with a Harley strapped upright turned into the gas station.

The RV: a beat-up old motor home, probably the owner's only house, aluminum sides cracked and dirty, little square windows with ragged drapes. When the driver stepped out, we could tell right away that the driver was a woman: tall, long-haired, jeans and a sweatshirt with a wolf airbrushed on the front. Instead of heading into the gas station, she came toward us. We waited. A window in the RV lit up orange, a shadow inside.

"Would you boys mind helping me out?"

"No ma'am," the guitarist said. "What can we do?"

I didn't know what to do with my beer. I chugged the rest of it, put the empty bottle down on the ground.

"I don't think the bike's on right. I can't set it right by myself."

The woman's voice was like the grit between my heel and the ground. The guitarist waved me over and the three of us went over to the trailer.

The woman said, "Someone needs to get up on the bike, make it steady."

The guitarist told me to, which I couldn't believe, I couldn't believe I was going to sit on the back of a Harley, it seemed like the cool job someone else would get. I stepped onto the trailer with a little more swagger than doing so required, but moved gingerly around the bike, afraid of the bike. When I sat on the seat, I set my feet firm on the wooden floor of the trailer, and said, "Okay."

In front of me was a little window, the little window you look at when you're driving behind a motor home and wonder about what's inside, only that night I could see straight in, and there was a red-haired girl seated at a chair in front of a mirror, at a little table. She wore a dirty white nightgown, and was doing something with her hair, pulling at it, long hair. She was twelve, I guessed, gawky-looking, her mouth open the way someone half asleep or daydreaming lets their mouth go slack.

I felt the bike jerk a little and tensed my legs.

"Okay," the woman said. "Thanks boys, that's a big help. I'd've been pretty sad if I lost that bike."

The drummer said, "It's a beauty."

I got off the trailer, a little dazed: I'd been intent on the shadowbox world the little girl lived in, bright orange and white. The world outside the box — the gas station, the acres of woods all around, the sky — was ridiculously huge.

The woman handed the guitarist some money, "You split that out between your friends."

We stepped back. The RV revved up, the orange lights in the back went out, and the woman and her bike and little girl were trundled out of the station. The guitarist handed me a twenty dollar bill. The drummer said, "Shit, she gave us sixty?"

Later, in the car on the way to the party in Martell, I said to the drummer, "There was a little red-haired girl in the RV. I saw her while I was up on the bike." The drummer and I were in the backseat, and he was being real quiet, which was odd because he was usually all gas and bluster.

The drummer asked, "You saw her naked?"

I said, "No. She was a little girl." Somehow that didn't clear things up quite right. So I said, "She kind of reminded me of your sister."

The drummer got quiet and I thought he was pissed off, like maybe he thought I was saying something about his sister, but before I could make to apologize, he said, loud so the guitarist could hear, "Shit, man, we shouldn't have taken the money." Before the guitarist could protest, the drummer added, "That was ignorant."

[PLATE 65]

"The Boating Party"

1894, 35½ x 46⅛

For anyone fond of water, and of color and of light—to say nothing of boats—we stay in a wonderful place. Our villa is on the water; from the porch I see snow-capped mountains and below them hills which can only be called rolling. Rather too panoramic for my taste, I wrote, and added that perhaps a great man could interpret the view satisfactorily. This is unusual, the inclusion of a male figure, who can occasionally be found in my sketches, but only rarely in finished works. That can be interpreted several ways.

All babies are different, so it only makes sense that all babies are born differently. And now you want to know, right, how you were born, a question all children eventually ask. I bet you don't realize what you're also asking. You're asking, "Where did I come from?" which is larger than, "How was I born?"

"I'm only asking how I was born, Mom."

"You're stubborn."

Key to your birth—*maybe* to the birth of some other children, but all I know for certain is what was essential to your birth—was color. Us and them, they say. Your father—I don't think he's told you this—was born without color or much size, for that matter, but you were a burst of colors, just the right number and concentration to make you.

On the day you were born your father said, "It's such a beautiful day, let's go for a row on the lake." What he meant by beautiful was colorful. Mostly blue.

Oh, daughter, no, look at that word, *blue*, hear it, mouth it and you'll only begin to sense what I mean. All you can really do is remember days when blue was at its varied best. When the prism of water plays with blue and the sky was a rainbow of blues and when even the trees in the distance — still green — shimmer blue in the breeze and hoard blue at their gnarled roots and in the rough grooves of their skin.

"Okay already, Mom. Could you just get to how I was born?"

"I know you're in a hurry but don't forget that most stories start before you know they have."

I was pregnant — with you, yes, in a way — anyhow, so I was a little reluctant to go to the lake since getting on and off a boat was tricky enough without my big fat belly and my balance all off.

You laugh, but one day, maybe, you too.

But your father was insistent and I didn't want to let him down and it was a beautiful day so we walked from the cottage down to the lake and to the end of the dock where your father's yellow and white rowboat was tethered, bopping kindly against the dock.

Your father, on some whim so unlike him, wore the scarf he was given by my mother, a blue scarf, but he wore it around his waist, like a cummerbund, except he wore it over his navy blue jacket, a wide band around his stomach and I've often thought that was partly why you were born when you were; that whim was why your birth worked the way it did.

I suppose you'd rather hear about my dress than about your father's clothes.

"No, not really, Mom."

"My dress was light blue with a hatch-work of thin brown lines and with a pattern of gold vines stitched into the jacket. I had a hat, too. The whole outfit was rather one of a kind and I was so pleased to have found something nice—when you're pregnant, clothes become an obstacle."

"Sounds wonderful, Mom."

"It was. Thank you."

Your father pushed off from the dock and was very handsome as he did it—he had a very well-kept beard back then, you know. As we rowed away from the deep green grass shore—they call it a sea of grass, when it looks like that—the air got cooler, which was a blessing because I was quite hot from carrying such a big baby.

"I wasn't a big baby!"

"No, you're right. You were perfectly normal in all respects."

Your father rowed us to the middle of the lake and once we were there—rising up and down—cooing is how I think of it—that was when I gave birth to you.

"In the middle of the lake?"

"Shh. Listen."

A fish, a trout I think—a rainbow trout?—hopped out of the lake and onto the boat, into the basket of my skirt. I nearly fell back out of the boat, I was so startled. And I let out a terrible scream. Your father leaned forward to save me from the fish that had leapt from the lake but as soon as he touched that fish—the instant his fingers made contact—the fish was a baby and that baby was you. There you were, fully dressed in a pink dress and matching hat that we still have to this day, kissing and sighing in my lap, a perfect baby, and I wasn't pregnant anymore—a little soft in the belly but half the size I was thank goodness. Your father and I laughed and we weren't in the least worried about getting back to the shore. Oh, your father picked up the oars from time to time and gave the boat a push, but mostly the current took us. Eventually the current took us home, carried us to the shore as a lioness carries her cub in her mouth—that is yellow, bright yellow and dark yellow and dusky yellow. Hot and lovingly yellow.

[PLATE 66]

"Children Playing on the Beach"

1884, 40 x 30¼

On the beach wearing winter jackets and hats. A bright yellow jacket, blue, a red plastic pail, all that sand, frozen, immovable but for the thinnest layer. Salt kept the ocean from freezing. Mom, Grandpa, our aunt. Leftovers from lunch in barn-shaped, cardboard boxes. Not a memory, but a picture that lives like a memory now.

Still children, Brother and Sister were sometimes left alone in the house. Frankly, before they were mature enough to be without parental guidance; but parents' lives make circumstances and so Brother and Sister sometimes came home to an empty house or stayed behind when Mom and Dad went

out.

And there were adventures when Mom and Dad left. Brother and Sister remember them all. Most took place in the living room with the television on.

Their house was small, the living room unimpressive. A faded blue couch. A record player with speakers. A bookshelf with a set of old encyclopedias full of stories true and not. The carpet was a woven oval, oval rings that served in Brother and Sister's imagination as roads and railroad tracks, rivers and ancient shore lines. When Brother and Sister shrank to the size of cherry pits, they spent their day on the carpet making the land.

To put it another way, even with the distraction of the television, even in a small room in a small house in a small town, Brother and Sister's adventures together were broad.

Sister enjoyed taking Brother to places where they'd been in the real world, places she remembered as somehow magic as

good.

A spring years before, Brother and Sister sat on the beach together with buckets and shovels and played without speaking, played as if in a trance. Sister proposed the carpet be the beach and the ocean, and Brother and Sister shrank themselves to the size of cherry pits and found themselves a suitable beach, grassy dunes behind, and the ocean — blue, gray, pink, white.

Sister said, "I see sailboats."

and

there were sailboats.

Brother tilted his head in their direction and the sailboats steered for the shore. When the sailboats arrived — hulls blue and barnacled like the back of a whale — Brother and Sister boarded. Where they were going they were not sure. On the horizon — a fuzzy, wavering carpet-line — was the coin dish; this the sailboats' course. But a change in the wind — a draft from under the front door — or perhaps on a whim, the sailboats edged left, toward the fireplace.

The hearth, once cold and gray-chalky, was now steaming; mist as from a volcano rose up into the chimney. Sister clutched Brother and pressed her face against his arm. He said, "We should be just fine."

And they were; they passed through the mist — warm and moist, yielding a clean, mineral smell — "We must have gone from ocean water to fresh." And indeed,

there were lake fish
all around the sailboats.

There, in the lake hearth, the mist behind Brother and Sister, the sailboats dropped anchor. Ahead of them was the brick back of the fireplace, a spot they'd stared at many times when Mom and Dad had lit a fire. Brother and Sister, lying on their stomachs, staring into the fire and then past the fire, at the flickering shadow-show.

From the deck of the sailboat Brother and Sister watched another shadow-show, and watched as the shadow-show dissolved and the bricks became a window or a mirror that showed a room. Mom and Dad were in that room. They were at a table, talking over cups of coffee. The cups were clear glass; steam shone above them. Brother and Sister's parents were talking, and Brother and Sister saw for the first time that their parents were friends who'd known each other for a long time, who loved each other as true friends do. In that, Brother and Sister saw they were like their parents

yet

because of their names — Brother. Sister. — they were more.

epilogue

"Portrait of the Artist"
1878, 24 x 18

My name is Mary and Mary is my museum. And what about the museum famous for being robbed? Not one great robbery; many robberies, great and otherwise. This museum, built at the turn of a century near a slow moving river in an old American city was robbed monthly and, briefly, daily, until it was empty. Now it's a museum of that.

On the book's jacket is an image of a tree, the tree she sees on her drive home, lit as it is at 3 A.M. The tree stands askew, angled away from the cemetery (roots firmly buried beneath). Behind the tree is a streetlight. Spring has come to the tree; its blossoms are yellow — gold at 3 A.M. The tree's trunk is black, haloed white. When she sees the tree on her drive home, she is in love with it. When she goes to bed, her exhaustion erases the tree. Strip the jacket from the book she holds; imprinted directly on the book's cloth cover is a gold silhouette of the tree on the jacket, of the tree she sees at 3 A.M.

The book is a story, but hidden inside that story are other stories, and these are the stories that matter to her, stories unworried about why the gold gears of their clockwork mesh. Let them mesh lovely, she thinks.

Dancing, for example, the little story about a dance that finishes with a kiss in the apartment with the wide plank wooden floors, the apartment built on such a slant that the two friends can't help but tumble together onto the couch. Where they deeply sleep. Behind the couch is an open window, and while during the night they are cold, the window yielded this reward: in the morning, before the sun, a branch blossomed and filled the room with a sweet smell that didn't wake the friends, but warmed them. All through the night they dreamed it rained; the rain was just the wind rolling the branch across the window-screen. How sleep can bloom happiness.

She relishes, too, when the friends meet again in a hotel room — just for one night. The little story begins: she must leave early; to stay the night is a great detour; she must leave early and yet he unpacks her bag, refolds her clothes and puts them into drawers. She protests: "I am leaving early tomorrow." He ignores her, unpacks, refolds. Finally she sees what he's doing and she smiles. She opens a window. She smokes from the sill, ashes into the garden below, the earth black and wet, her ashes, dry. The flowers that grow in that garden are shut tight; frogs call from a pond. He pours her a glass of water from the tap. "Here," he says. "Drink this." She does. He's been living in the hotel room for weeks. He forgets, sometimes, where he is. She drove 100 miles out of her way to visit and they remind each other that had things been different — and the bed glows, all white, crisply made, lit by a fluorescent bulb mounted on the headboard. "I have to leave early," she says, and lights another cigarette.

The story rolls on, the book does, the book carried the friends apart for a year, more, months, weeks, a day, they are together again. She who reads the book loves when the friends come together.

The friends have done so much. He's tired. She's worse. At night — the brick sidewalks are rain-wet, shine under streetlights, reflect the black branches of trees not yet in bloom. "Here, let me show you something," she says, and he follows her, his friend, down a quiet street, to a little green house. The sky is empty, black, smooth and glossy: a fingernail across the sky would leave a silver line. "I'm always tired," he says. His friend lights a cigarette, takes his hand and they walk into the backyard of the little green house. "Have a puff," she says, and he takes her cigarette, though he does not ordinarily smoke, and he adds this intimacy between them to his list. He is light-headed, breaks out into a sweat, then is cool again. "Here," she says. A family plot, a few headstones. At the center of the plot is a tree, and it is gold. At the base of the tree is a statue of Mary, hands palm up. "Mary says she loves us," he says. The friends hold hands. They step close to the tree and smell its bark. Sweet, damp. She drops her cigarette; the wet ground snuffs it out with a hiss. The friends inhale, deeply. They lean their backs against the tree. Before dawn — the birds go mad — the friends have disappeared, absorbed by the golden tree.

She puts the book down. She marvels that the tree from the book grows so close to her house, grows askew, its roots deep among graves.

about the author

Adam Golaski is the author of *Worse Than Myself* (Raw Dog Screaming Press, 2008). He is a founder of Flim Forum, a press publishing books of contemporary experimental poetry, and is the editor of *New Genre*, a literary journal for new and experimental horror and science fiction.